The Trials of Ann Rumsby

Brian Hungerford

The Trials of Ann Rumsby

Bonnet v Teapot

The Trials of Ann Rumsby
ISBN 978 1 76109 300 5
Copyright © text Brian Hungerford 2022
Cover image: *Lady Blackwood*, by George Gregory, public domain,
from commons.wikimedia.org

First published 2022 by
GINNINDERRA PRESS
PO Box 3461 Port Adelaide 5015
www.ginninderrapress.com.au

1

The First Trial

Ann stood in the dock, squirming about, shifting her weight from foot to foot, too hungry, too grubby, too itchy and too far gone for anything else. She had a gnawing urge to rear back her head and to use all her strength to whip forward again and send a throat load of phlegmy spit at the idiot-looking judge who was droning on at her. But he was too far away. She was desperate to do something. But nothing seemed possible.

Ann felt sick just looking at the judge. Everything about him was wrong. He spoke with the high-pitched shriek of a market woman. He didn't even look like a man. He looked more like a woman who'd let herself go; a woman who didn't know how to dress herself. He sat up there under a huge wooden canopy, wearing a grubby wig big enough to house a whole family of mice. 'How can such a creature tell me anything?'

She watched the butler down there in front of the judge, fussing about, whispering to the policeman. The policeman craned up and whispered in turn to the judge. The judge simply rocked his head, up and down, as if in disgusted belief. She heard the policeman use the word whore. The butler nodded and the judge looked at Ann as something of a grubby maggot that could spoil his lunch.

Ann heard the words of disgust from the judge. He said nothing about the bonnet. She heard him praise the wonderful work of the butler and she heard praise for the policemen who had had to use extreme force to arrest her. She almost smiled at his advice that seven years in New South Wales would serve to mend her ways and enable her to return to Norfolk as a worthwhile member of society. Seven years! It was almost half her life already. She saw the butler smile at the policeman who turned and bowed to the judge like the judge was some sort of bishop. While she stood in shock, a policeman snatched at her arm and pulled her from the dock and down the steps to the cells below.

And so that day in Norfolk, a new era of Australian history was born. The birth was via a virgin English girl, allegedly of seventeen or eighteen years.

On that day, Ann Rumsby, an illiterate serving girl was sentenced to seven years transportation to Botany Bay. Neither Ann Rumsby nor Australia would ever be the same again

But the new Australian era didn't progress much on that day, or the next, or over the next few days after that; or even after her move to a dirtier prison near London. For the next few weeks in the new jail, she heard countless tales of innocence and misery, of women selling their bodies for a mouthful of bread, of licking men, all over, for the offer of a bed.

In her overcrowded cell, Ann fought a rat from her plate before she ate. She looked forward to Botany Bay.

According to a few of the other women, Botany Bay was a beautiful place, just off the south coast of France. She was told that lots of women went there, but not many came back because the colony made them so happy. She was sceptical, but she knew it had to be better than what she had.

What did concern her was the talk of so few coming back. She knew that no place was so wonderful that no one ever wanted out. Even Lucifer wanted out from Heaven. And he used to be up there, living the life of Riley, of everlasting luxury, lovely blue skies all around him, free food, gorgeous free clothes, no work, just pleasure everlasting up there in Heaven. Ann would enjoy Heaven. She'd be able to hang about the Pearly Gates waiting for the butler to arrive. But then again he might not arrive. He might go down to the Other Place because of all his lies. In a way, that would be a pity. She would enjoy a few serious words with him. After that, he could get himself carted off below for being wicked.

Apart from the rat-infested, freezing cells and disgusting food, Ann wasn't particularly unhappy in jail. She waited for shipment to New South Wales and the everlasting blue skies and French food. Lots of the women talked about places called either Botany Bay, New South Wales or Port Jackson. Ann only knew that she was to go to Botany Bay. A few of the women said all three places were the same place and it was only different judges who used different names. Several women informed her that the worst place was called Van Diemen's Land. In that place, the local people were said to be brutal and hated anyone English, and the only language convicts were allowed to speak was Dutch. If you didn't learn Dutch quick smart, you just starved to death and they fed what was left of you to the pigs. How these women knew all these things Ann couldn't fathom. In the meantime, she shared her food with rats and her blanket with bedbugs and learned new songs from a music hall singer who'd fallen on hard times.

At the end of November, Ann was moved to London, then to Portsmouth and finally, on Christmas Day 1821, she was shackled to other women and clanged up the gangplank onto a ship called the *Mary Anne*. At the wharf end of the gangplank there was a mishmash of scurry and confusion. An officer sat at a small table on the wharf and demanded of each prisoner to know her name and conviction. Ann agreed to everything and signed her name with a cross. The sailor then ordered another sailor to hand her a rolled-up blanket, two wooden bowls and a wooden spoon. She was then shuffled down with other women to the prison deck below. To Ann, it seemed they had to go down, deck after deck. One of the middle decks was so low she had to bend forward and stumble in her chains. In the darkest part of the ship, iron bars had been installed to make the whole deck into two cells, one on each side of the ship. Two sailors stood at the cell door and unfastened the shackles. Some of the chains took time to undo. The locks were rusty.

At the back end of the ship, more light filtered down from hatches.

In the front there was very little light and the women had to grope about finding the limits of their space. The ship had been scrubbed and fumigated, but still stunk of rotting dead rats and evidence that several people had already squatted and half-filled the slop bucket. The women were disgusted to find that the only toilet was nothing more than one big wooden bucket at the darkest end of the cell.

The woman next to Ann commented, 'It's easy to fill up, but how do we empty it out?'

Ann couldn't bring herself to wonder. She already felt sick and the thought of trying to vomit into a bucket already half full brought a re-flux of vomit up into her throat. She managed to keep it down. 'Thank God the voyage will only last a few days. With a bit of luck, I can also put up with constipation and go to the toilet when we get off in Botany Bay.'

The women were ordered to lie down in rows, under swinging ham-mocks. At least they had the luxury choice of lying on their back or belly. They lay there chatting in the dark and some shouted for food. One group had not eaten in three days.

'It's the luck of the draw,' said the older woman next to Ann.

After what seemed hours in the dark, none of the women were sleeping until there was a jolt and they felt the ship heave. The boards beneath them seemed to move backwards and forwards. There was a surge as the girls lifted where they lay and a few women began to cry in fear. One woman screamed that they were going to sink arse-first, and they'd all be slowly drowned.

A sailor walked into the aisle between the cells and shouted the in-formation that the ship was being towed out into the road. 'We're being towed by rowing boats,' he shouted. 'When we're out in the right road, we'll go under sail. There's nothing to worry about.' He didn't wait for any questions, but turned on his heel and left.

Ann wondered about the word road. Was there a road under the waves? She didn't believe that ships had wheels. Why was the man talk-ing about roads?

Gradually the surging of the ship increased and within another hour, the women felt a heaving shudder as the ship's sails flopped unfurled. The ship lurched and humped as if alive. Many of the women began to scream and swear their innocence before Almighty God and say that no court had the right to banish them from their own country. Ann lay uncomfortable. She had not washed, even her face, since her day in court and the woman beside her had not washed any part of her body for more than a year. The older woman on the other side of her wailed and urinated where she lay. The smell of vomit, urine, faeces and bleeding brought on heaving nausea throughout the group. Within an hour of the ship being under way, Ann threw up what she had eaten that morning. She almost laughed at her discovery that the food was warmer on the way up than it had been on the way down.

Nothing new happened the first day, or on the first night. The ship groaned and squeaked, swung about like a great lumbering pig in mud, and the women were swung about, crashing into each other. Many vomited. Ann prayed quietly that the journey to Botany Bay, or whatever the place was called, would not take too many days. For a moment, there was a short refocus when a sailor came below to look over the convicts and perhaps to take his pick. He didn't stay long, but retreated from the foul smell.

The next morning, the sea was calm and the women were ordered up on deck where they were ordered to wash from buckets of seawater. Their ablutions done, they returned below to wash the deck and to clean up any solid matter. An officer then arrived below and gave a string of orders and voiced the hope that they would have an easy journey on the *Mary Anne*. He advised that if any sickness occurred, their spokeswoman would have to inform the officer on duty and medical help would be at hand. He explained that the ship had an excellent doctor, James Hall, who was considerate to their situation. If they were well behaved, they would be permitted on deck as much as possible and as they sailed south, the sun itself would ease any sickness and banish their fear of the dark.

He also advised that any woman who caused trouble would be taken on deck, stripped naked and flogged. 'The severity of the punishment will be measured according to the misbehaviour,' he said. He also passed on the medical information that convict women on the ship should not worry about menstruation. He recited, 'Your cycle of female periods on a monthly basis will not happen until you reach your destination. After a few weeks on land, eating fresh food rations, your old friend and nuisance will return as per normal. In the meantime, keep yourself clean. Keeping clean is the best defence against rats trying to eat your hair at night. If you don't keep washed, rats will attack you both day and night. As we reach the tropics, swarms of insects will crawl out of the timbers and constantly try to eat you. Their attacks will ease off when we again enter cold seas. Tomorrow, or the next day, Doctor Hall will visit you all and anyone suffering from any catchy sort of disease will be isolated. He will also conduct health checks on every convict. To do that, you must obey his every command.' As a final comment, he informed the women that the voyage would last for somewhere between four and five months. He turned, covered his nose with a cloth and left.

His last words stopped Ann thinking of anything. She thought of nothing other than his words about four or five months. Those words clanged in her head like a cracked church bell. The clanging rattled her entire body and she heard, or felt, nothing from anyone. Silence spread over all the women like a smelly blanket. No one spoke, or moved, until one of the younger girls began to sob. Ann was no longer that young and she was past sobbing.

That night, Ann lay numb. She wasn't sickened by the smell or afraid of the dark, or of wanting to continue any sort of life. She knew she wasn't alive any more. There would be no Botany Bay, no French food and wine, no dreams even. She had moved into one of the levels of Hell, a Hell of no fire or even warmth, just a level of the putrid smell of rats and the stinking decay of human beings who couldn't even clean up after using the slop bucket and she knew that the punishment of four or five months at sea was more than any girl could survive.

'Tonight, I start a new life,' she said to herself. 'I will play dead until we reach the land. I will live in the dark belly of the *Mary Anne* and I will only know another day when the women at the back start shouting that the sun has come up again. Tomorrow, I will think of something. I don't know or care what it might be. But I'll think of something. I might get Sally to write a letter to the butler and tell him I'm having a wonderful time and it's him I have to thank for organising me free trip. I'll tell him to be more careful than he was before or he'll get some terrible sickness from the street girls he knows.' Ann almost smiled. 'I'll even do better and have Sally write to my last mistress and ask her to be careful with the butler and not to be cross when she hears that he plays with his spout in the park.'

Ann went to sleep with a smile. She was starting to feel better already.

2

Doctor James Hall

The sun was coming up. The women down-ship were shouting about daytime and the cooks were rattling pots and shouting swear words. A bell was ringing and Ann had worked it out that the bell told her that it was four in the morning. Ann had learned the day before that the bell rang with eight chimes, at eight, four and twelve o'clock. It rang once for the half-hours. It was still pitch-dark in the cell, but she had slept through many commotions of the night. Soon there was shouting from the sailors and crashing thumping somewhere on the main deck.

Half an hour later, a sailor walked between the cells shouting orders that the women must prepare themselves for a washing. He shouted the orders over and over until one of the women asked him to join her in the cell so that she could wash his head in the slop bucket.

Preparation didn't mean much. The women were already barefooted, wore the same jacket, day and night, and tried to keep clean, washing where they slept and learning to wash their face and hands with only a drinking mug of fresh water.

An older woman had advised the girls that the important job of keeping yourself clean was to remember the three Fs. 'You got to look after your face, your feet and your fanny. The rest of you looks after itself.'

Despite the public routine on deck, Ann looked forward to even a good wash with a bucket of seawater. But this time it was different. The women assembled in the half light on deck with the hint of a pale dawn somewhere in front of the ship. The breeze was strong, with the sails lifting the ship through the water. The breeze was cold, but it was such a delicious change from the smell and the darkness below. A big tub, shaped like a coffin, was hauled across the deck by two sailors and the first girl was ordered to strip. She screamed that she had done nothing wrong and why should she be flogged. The sailors simply laughed and pulled her tunic up over her head. She stood there naked in the pre-dawn, her left arm across her chest and the right hand trying to cover her secret bit below. One sailor whistled his approval of her body. Several sailors stood about trying to look busy, but enjoying the free strip show.

Ann stood with the other women watching this new bullying game, wanting to intervene, but not understanding how such a situation could arise. The naked girl was ordered to lie in the tub. She scrambled in and lay face down. A sailor hauled a bucket from the sea and poured it over her back. She squealed from the cold, but lay still. A second sailor wielded the long-handled wicker broom. As the first sailor hauled up more water, the broomer began to sweep and scrub the girl's back. He paid particular attention to the girl's buttocks, scrubbing out dried mess from the cleavage. She was then ordered to turn over and more water and more scrubbing on her front was watched by the assembled crowd of sailors and convicts. The girl hauled herself out of the tub, sobbing, and tried to dry herself with a strip of canvass.

Ann went next. She stripped and held her nose waiting for the freezing seawater and the stiff broom. On order, she turned over and after one bucket full on her belly she was ordered to stand. She felt shame but thankful to have an almost clean body. It was such a change from the smell she'd carried about since her day in court.

The scrubbing on her front also revealed that the officer's advice from the day before was inaccurate. She was having a period. In desperation, she stood in the tub while the sailor threw a bucket of water over her belly to wash the blood down and then another to get the blood from her legs. A nod from the first sailor and she stepped out of the tub and two sailors emptied the water from the tub onto the deck.

Ann felt a strange surge of pride. 'I'm still a girl. I'm bleeding to prove it. I'm going to win this silly boys' game. They can strip me bollocky in public, but they can't win me over.'

The girl next to her leaned in and asked, 'What you got to smile about?'

'It's because I'm still here,' she answered.

The bosun ordered two of the women at the back to start scrubbing and cleaning the deck. Ann shivered from the cold, but was smiling within herself. 'I'm still a girl,' she kept saying to herself as she bent forward to wipe traces of blood from the inside of her left leg. By the time she was dry, some twenty of the women had been scrubbed and the whole group were then herded below again and divided into groups of six.

Ann tore strips from her under-petticoat and plaited the strips into a rough knot with a length of cotton thread, tying in each end till she had what looked like an engorged sausage. Then she used a length of string around her waist and two more shorter pieces, one for the front and the other down between the cheeks of her bottom, to hold the wad in place and soak up the blood. The Irish woman helped her adjust the string from the back so that the wad wouldn't slip about. The two of them talked about how they might wash the blood from her new wad.

'We'll have to think of something,' the Irishwoman said. 'This is going to happen four or five times before we get to where we're going.'

At eight bells, one woman from each group went to the ship's galley to collect rations. Each returned with an armload of biscuits and a pot of gruel with sugar. The same woman shared the gruel into six bowls and a bit more for herself, on account of her having to carry it all. She also brought a keg of water with the advice that each convict was entitled to almost three quarts of water each day. Ann's first mug of fresh water went to washing the salt water from her face.

The women set to, eating biscuit and gruel with their wooden spoons and taking turns to drink from the horn tumbler. They ate in the dark. Ann knew she could cope with the dark, but already she yearned to be back on deck in the clean air. Even if it meant the cruel scrubbing.

Breakfast over, a sailor came down with a flaming torch to light up the whole cell block. He ordered the women to start scrubbing. Two more sailors brought buckets of seawater and a collection of flat stones. It was just a case of dipping the stones in the water and scrubbing the floor. Two of the biggest women lifted and carried the slop bucket up all the steps to the deck. The bosun tied a length of rope to the bucket and helped the women tip the contents into the sea. The women threw the bucket overboard, hauled it back full of water and scrubbed the inside with a flat stone. They tipped it back and repeated the filling and cleaning until the bosun was satisfied.

The bosun swore at them for taking so long and threatened to hit them across the back with a length of heavy rope. 'All you want is a holiday up on deck. You'll spend all day up there pretending to work. I'm awake up to you lot. Any more hanging about and it'll be a flogging, understand?'

The two women chuckled and told him what he could do with his flogging and if he was so worried, they could demonstrate to him just where they would shove his bucket as well. He took a swipe at them with the rope – which they ducked. They didn't wait any longer, but went off laughing with their almost clean bucket.

Ann's Irish friend, who slept two women farther along, scratched about in her bed roll in the dark. Soon she gave a grunt of satisfaction and started to say a prayer in Irish. 'Well,' thought Ann, 'It must be Irish – what other language is there?' But she liked the lilting sound of it all. It sounded more like the words of a song than a prayer.

The prayer in the dark came to an end followed by a soft blowing sound and then the Irish woman began to play a penny whistle. At first, she played an Irish tune that silenced all the women and then, after a breath, she began to play a tune that all the women knew. It was the most popular song in most of the music halls in London and up and down the country. She played on and soon several of the women joined in singing. Gradually, all the women were singing. Ann knew the song was about a convict girl and the women sang it out as though it had become their own anthem. They sang it out full blast as their private challenge.

When the Irishwoman finished, there was resounding applause and calls for more. The cheers were cut short when three men came below. The young officer in front was followed by two sailors who each carried a cudgel. The women turned silent waiting for something to happen. The officer stopped where he could be vaguely seen and looked around at all the prisoners.

'Looks like he's got good eyesight,' chuckled one of the women.

The officer took no notice, but raised his hand for silence. 'My name is James Hall,' he said. 'I am the ship's surgeon and it is my responsibility to ensure that you all land in Hobart and Sydney fit and healthy – ready for work. I am not interested in why you are here, or what you might have done. Your souls are in the hands of God. Your bodies and your good health are, with God's help, in my hands. I cannot examine you down here. However, I will have you all, but one or two at a time, taken to the ship's sickbay for a thorough check. If one of you has any worry, like a rash, or blisters, or painful discharges, even the fear of an illness or injury, you must tell me when you arrive at the sickbay.'

He started to turn, but stopped. 'I will begin examinations tomorrow after breakfast and clean-out. We will start with the older, married women.' And with that he turned round, covered his nose with a cloth and left.

There was a long silence after he left until one of the women laughed and said there was something about the man – that he seemed very handsome.

An older woman snorted, 'Handsome is as handsome does.'

Another woman made a comment that the young doctor clearly wanted to be on the side of God.

Another woman said, 'I don't know if God lives in New South Wales. I've heard that God doesn't exist once you get more than three miles off the south coast of England. But just the same, they say the doctor wants to stay on in Sydney. So some girl's going to be lucky.'

'Where's Sydney? A girl asked.

'It's two or three streets away from Botany Bay,' the first woman informed. 'But wherever it is, it'll be better than rotting out our lives down here in the arse-end of the *Mary Anne*.'

Most of the women, including Ann agreed with that. However, she couldn't help but wonder how the other prisoners knew so much about the doctor. The only thing that rang a bell for her was his mention that the women's souls were in the hands of God. 'God seems very important to him,' she mumbled to herself. 'I hope God isn't so important in Botany Bay. The butler was always talking about God. But for all his love of God, it didn't stop him causing trouble. So why didn't God step in and stop the butler telling all them lies and getting me put on the *Mary Anne*? I don't think you can trust God. Not if you can't read and write anyway. God looks after them what knows a thing or two. The rest of us will have to look after ourselves.'

That afternoon, after a meal of a lump of cooked pork each, a fistful of bread and a bowl of pea soup, a storm blew up. A sailor came to the cells and the women were ordered into their hammocks and told not to worry.

'This storm won't last,' he said. 'It's always rough in these waters. We're heading near the Bay of Biscay on the run down to Brazil. By tomorrow morning, we should be shot of all this.' Then he laughed and said in a softer voice that if any of the younger girls were frightened, he could always come down and he would look after one or two.

The convict women scoffed and assured him that if he so wished, one or two of them would come up on deck and grab him by the spout and throw him over the side where the sharks would look after his body and soul. The man retreated laughing.

Ann smiled. 'At least there are men here who can laugh. None of them laughed in prison. And the butler never laughed.' But she didn't smile for long. Nor did she muse much longer on her life on the *Mary Anne*.

The next morning, which was not much of a morning, the women began moving about, taking turns at the slop bucket and complaining of the cold. With no light and no clocks, the women listened for the ship's bell. By remembering the last ring, they knew the time, though they were never sure if it was day or night. Their marker of dawn was eight bells followed by the swearing and banging noises from the cooks starting work.

More than their hunger for food, the women hungered for the smell of the open sea and the clean wind on their faces. Time passed slowly as they thought about a scrubbing on deck and feeling clean again. The salt water needed to be rinsed off, but such a luxury was not available. The women would try every trick they knew to stay on deck longer, to feel human again, but nothing worked. The bosun would deliver a few thumps, with his half a yard of rope, and the women would return into the blackness below.

After breakfast, and their scrubbing on deck, the women returned to the cells to be met by two sailors who demanded two older women for their first inspection in the sickbay. They weren't gone long and on their return all the girls gathered around hoping for good news. Actually, any news would have done. They were interrupted by the same two sailors coming to take another two women.

The second pair was brought back even quicker than the first two and with the same news.

'We're not much use to him, I'm afraid,' the oldest one said. 'But just the same, it was nice to lie on a proper sort of bed.'

'What did he do?' Ann asked.

'Nothing much, just the usual purvey doctor things.'

'Like what?' Ann asked again.

'Well, you have to strip off and lie down. Then he, well, I think he's a member of the Wandering Hands Society, well, he quickly runs his hands over the top of your body, feels your neck, looks down your throat, taps your teeth, all that stuff. Then he has his two offsiders grab a leg each and you're stretched open. The doctor spends most of his time crouching down and looking up inside you as best he can. He's got a special tool like a blunt pair of scissors. He sticks that in and opens you up.'

Several women asked if it hurt.

'Not much. If you wriggle about, one of the sailors gives you a bit of a knuckling on your shoulder. If you just lie there, you'll be right.'

One woman asked, 'But what's he looking for?'

'Just to see if you got something in there.'

'What do you mean something?'

'He's probably looking for folded money in an oilskin. But mostly he's looking for signs of some sort of sickness. He wants to know how long since you been with a man. And he asks things like, did you do it for money, that sort of thing.'

Another girl seemed frightened and asked, 'How can he be sure we haven't got something? Some sort of terrible sickness down there, we might have got from men.'

'He'll know. He's probably seen plenty of that.'

Ann listened and wondered what it was that a girl could get down there. She knew there was no possibility that there could be something. 'Thank God I never been with a man,' she said to herself.

But the older woman wanted to talk on. 'And I tell you this, don't get him upset. If you do, he'll give you a terrible hard time. He can put you on a work party, in shackles, scrubbing decks and washing clothes for the officers. And it's best you speak highly of God. That man just loves God. I couldn't help laughing. There I was laying there with me legs stretched out and wide open. Them two sailors is there all the time, one on each of me legs. And there's the doctor crouching down so he can get a good look up inside me. He was so close, I was frightened he was going to bite me. Some men do. But all the time he was fumbling about with his fingers inside me thing and blathering on about God and asking me how many times a day I says me prayers. The trouble is I couldn't talk for laughing. He was angry and I could feel his hot breath on me quim. He says I was a blasphemer or something. I couldn't stop a sort of a giggle and I says to him what he shouldn't try to talk with his mouth full. He went off over that. What a temper. He spat in me quim. He stood up and gives one of the sailors a nod. That was the end of the inspection. But not before the sailor hauled off and fisted me on the side of me face. I was groggy after that and the two sailors dressed me and half carried me out and back here. So take it from me. Just play along and say you loves God. Tell him something like you'll never do nothing, never again, with any man. Tell him that anything you do do, you'll only do it for God.'

By the middle of the afternoon, most of the older women had been to the doctor. They all told the same story. From then on, Doctor Hall was called Dr Sticky Fingers.

The next morning, things were different for Ann Rumsby. She was taken up on her own. The women tried to warn her.

'He was up early this morning. He took a lot of interest in your bath,' one woman said.

'You'll be all right,' one said. 'He's frightened of whores.'

Ann wanted to shout back that she wasn't a whore, but she bit the words back. She knew that some of the women were, in fact, whores. But talking in a crowd, all the women swore they were virgins. Even a couple of the married ones.

The sailor took her by the elbow and pushed her up the ladder onto the open deck, then had her walk to the back of the ship and into a cabin on the port side. It was small; the walls were covered by shelves with bottles secured by their tops. She was ordered to strip and lie on a table. The doctor came in and ordered the sailor to get another helper. While the escort sailor was gone, the doctor looked over her upper body. Examined her teeth and explored her neck with his fingers. He pushed her breasts about with his thumbs for some time.

'That hurts,' she complained. She knew it didn't hurt, but she'd never had anyone pushing her about like that, and the thought of being something to be played with was worse than pain.

'Silence!' ordered the doctor. 'I'll tell you when it hurts.'

'Am I supposed to say thank you for me being played with?'

'I can see you are not conditioned to keeping the peace.'

'I'm sure you can see anything you likes.' Ann would have said more had his hands not started to wander down her belly. 'What you looking for?'

'Any sign of illness.'

'Well, that won't be hard. I been sick ever since I got on this big boat. I been throwing up three and four times a day and I can't keep any food down more than half an hour or so.'

'Why didn't you complain?'

'What's the odds? Them other women would only cause me more trouble.'

'That's what convicts are good at.'

Ann might have replied, but the soft sensation of his fingers on her upper thigh silenced her. She immediately clamped her knees together.'

'Don't be afraid,' he said gently. 'It is my duty to examine the workings of every convict woman on this ship. So just do as you are told and that'll be the end of all your trouble.' His voice then took on the voice of command and he ordered the two sailors to do their job.

Each sailor grabbed a leg each, and with all their strength, they stretched her legs wide apart. She tried to fight back, but one sailor slapped her across the face with his open hand. Her vision blurred and she collapsed within herself. She came to when she felt her private parts being dug into. She craned her head up to see what has happening. She could feel what was happening, but didn't want to believe it. She felt the doctor withdraw one or two fingers and saw his head down between her thighs as if he were looking for something.

'Convict?' he said with a puzzled voice. 'According to the list, you are a thief and whore. Yet I see you are still a virgin. All your tissue is still intact. Have you been having sex up the back passage?'

'I never in all my life have anyone ask me anything like that. And I am no whore. I was never a whore and I never done nothing with any man or boy. On top of that, I was never a thief. I was tricked with all them lies onto this ship with all them criminal women. You are the only man who ever touched me down there, and if you ever touch me like that again, I will kill myself. Next time we go for a wash, I will just jump over the side into the sea. By the time someone tries to save me, I will be dead.'

Ann watched like a caged animal as the doctor wiped his hands on a rag. She was in pain from the sailors holding her knees apart. 'And Doctor Hall,' she asked, 'please make these monkeys let go of me. I'm not going to jump up and run away.'

The doctor nodded to the two sailors. They released her legs, He nodded again and both sailors left with hungry looks at her naked body.

As soon as they were gone, the doctor took her tunic from the bench and handed it to her. 'Get yourself dressed and we'll discuss your situation.'

Ann threw the tunic over her head and sat on the edge of the bench. 'What situation?'

'Convict Rumsby, whether you are innocent or not is a moot point. But you must control your tongue. And to start with, you must stop asking non-stop questions. Now, let us put all that behind us and you tell me, without any qualifications, how sick you are.'

'Terrible sick.'

'And how sick is terrible sick?'

'Really, terrible terrible sick.'

'Then if you could control yourself I might be able to help you.'

'How's that then?'

'Well, it might help you if you were not down there in the dark with all those other convicts.'

She was about to say something cheeky when he put his hand up ordering her to be quiet.

'Ann,' he said, using her name for the first time, 'I cannot give you freedom on the *Mary Anne*, but I can help you in New South Wales.' He sat next to her and almost nervously touched her hand. 'You are a beautiful girl and you don't deserve what has happened. And I know you will be fearful of any man trying to win your heart.'

'Most of them don't aim that high.'

He ignored her joke. 'I am going to make a suggestion.'

'I hope that's not followed by your fingers. You doing that hurt me and I feel ashamed that I can't rip your arms off, just to get even. So I have to sit here and listen to you jawing on as if you was my friend. What do you want me to do?'

'Well, to start with, I believe you. And because you seem to be innocent of any crime and because you are surrounded by, shall we say, the dregs of Mother England, I am determined to improve your conditions.'

'How?'

'I won't do anything if you don't stop asking questions. However, you will return to the cells and tomorrow morning you have to vomit after breakfast.'

'That'll be easy. Everything I eat down there makes me want to vomit. So what then?'

'I will have you brought up here again and I will consider having you transferred to the sickbay. The food will be marginally better and you will have access to sunlight and a more comfortable bed.'

'Why all this then?'

'Because I believe in your cause. I feel it my Christian duty to take care of you. Now, off you go.' He breathed heavily for a few moments, stood up and tapped loudly three times on the table.

At that, the two sailors returned, grabbed her arms and marched her down into the gloom of the cells.

On the way down, the two sailors chuckled about the word conversion. 'He's got a pretty good converter. They reckon his converter's very long. So, convict, you're in for an exciting trip out. I hope you like it. We call him Fanny Fingers.'

Ann pretended not to understand. But already she perfectly understood her new situation. She knew that however her life might run would depend on her handling of the ship's surgeon. 'Oh, Mum,' she said to herself, why aren't you here to help me when I needs you? Everyone needs a mum sometimes and. I badly needs you right now.'

3

Doctor Fanny Fingers

Dr Hall was true to his word. On the dying clang of eight bells on the morning following her first medical encounter, the bosun's whistle shrilled through the deck followed by the sounds of men hauling something across the deck above them.

Moments later, two sailors arrived ordering the women on deck for their bath. The ritual was the same, except that many of the women actually looked forward to getting cleaned up. The ship stank of unwashed bodies and human excrement. The day was starting to warm, much more so than the day before and she drank in the sight of blue skies and a blue ocean.

The first girl screamed again that she didn't want to strip off in public, that her mother would have thrashed her for doing such a thing.

'Good old mum,' grunted the older sailor with a bit of a laugh. He'd heard it all before. He scratched the top of her head.

She flung her arms up in defence and at that moment the second sailor bent forward, grabbed the hem of her tunic and ripped it off over her head in one easy movement. The watching sailors cheered. The girl gave up and sobbed as she stepped naked into the bath box and lay belly down waiting for the scrubbing. Another sailor emptied a bucket of seawater over her back and the brooming man went to work. His stiff broom scratched her back and again he paid attention to the cleavage of her bottom.

Ann was next again. She undid her home-made period pad, stripped herself naked and stepped into the tub. The seawater was freezing and added to the salty sting from the day before. It was as if the doctor's fingers had never been withdrawn, and she clamped her thighs together.

'Stand up,' shouted the sailor and Ann did so.

The second sailor threw a bucket of water over her belly and swore. Ann looked down. At first she felt shame, but soon felt a flush of a small victory. A small stream of blood still trickled past her knee waiting for another bucket of water to wash it down.

'Take it easy, woman, and put your feet apart. Nothing's gunna fall out,' the older sailor said.

Both men laughed. Ann didn't understand the joke and stepped out of the tub to fold herself in a sheet of worn sailcloth.

The next woman took her place and Ann retreated to the waiting group. She began to shiver, but didn't want to drag her dry tunic over her wet body. One of the women rubbed her with the canvas to dry her as best she could. For all their efforts, the wind dried her off better than the canvas and after a short while she could rearrange her pad and put her tunic on again. She felt safe. She remembered that as a serving girl she had only seldom worn underpants, but there in Norfolk she had worn long dresses and sometimes two heavy petticoats on top. That life now seemed a pleasant dream from some other childhood ages ago.

By the time half the women were scrubbed down, there was not much more to see. The sailors were sick of the job and the bosun sent all the women below to scrub out before breakfast. Ann was happy to join them, though an hour or so on deck with the clean air would have been delicious.

The women scrubbed the deck in the cells, emptied the slop bucket and waited for the call to collect their food. Their monitor heard the call, hurried off and within minutes returned with the biscuits, along with bowls of thin soup and clean water. In the dim light, the women examined each biscuit, broke each one in half and shook the biscuit into the other hand. A few maggots fell out. The women kept breaking and shaking until all the maggots were out and thrown into the bucket.

Ann smiled to herself as she wondered if the maggots enjoyed their new, if temporary home. She wondered if they were happy being warm and wet. For all that, the biscuit taste was next to revolting, but better than nothing. Ann ate one biscuit and hid the second for later.

No sooner had she forced the last of the biscuit down than a sailor walked in and called out for 'Convict Rumsby.' Even in the dim light, Ann recognised him as one of the sickbay sailors. A coldness over all her body warned her that her almost planned moment of salvation, or the reverse, was about to start. She knew she had to begin an action. How and what to do she had no idea and she trembled slightly as she fell in step behind the sailor.

The sailor seemed to run up the ladders. Ann hurried as best she could and once on deck she breathed in the clean salty air. A sailor was coiling rope on the deck and he smiled at her. She smiled back. It wasn't the most sensible thing to do.

'Off to see Fanny Fingers, are we?' he said quietly.

She looked out at the sea, pretending she hadn't heard a single word.

'Let's know what he's like – if you can still walk – on your way back.' He said this a bit louder and a string of sailors, hauling the big sail higher, all laughed.

Ann followed the sickbay sailor to the port side of the ship. They hurried along the deck to a nest of cabin doors under the aft deck. The first door led to the doctor's rooms and sickbay. The sailor knocked and stood back. The door opened and she saw Doctor Hall standing just inside. He waved her in without looking up from his papers, stepped across and shut the door.

'I'm here,' she said. 'Your man called me.'

Still without looking up, he seemed to growl. 'I'll tell you when to speak,' he barked at her.

'My God,' she thought. 'He growls and he barks. I think he's half dog.'

Why are you smiling?' he demanded, looking up at her face. 'And tell me, have you vomited today?'

'Only after what you lot calls breakfast.'

The doctor looked around as if searching for something to support his medical interests. 'Sorry to hear that.' He waved her towards the bed.

Ann moved to the side of the bed and stood stiff.

'I'm told you are a very impudent convict.'

'I don't know what one of them things is. But I was brought up with the love of God.'

The doctor frowned, as if, for a moment, guilty of something, But he quickly changed to annoyance, which changed to anger. 'You didn't reply to my accusation. Are you impudent?'

'If I knew about that, I would tell you. All I know is that I depend on the love of God.'

'Who told you to say that?'

'No one told me to say nothing. But I was told to be careful of you.'

'Then you are not only impudent, but a troublemaker. Do you re-alise that I could have you flogged for statements like that.'

'I'm sure you could.'

'Well, then, recant.'

'Is that a swear word? Anyway, I will have to do what pleases them upstairs. I'm a convict and you is a doctor, upstairs.'

The doctor struggled inside himself, his eyes fixed on Ann's body. It was moments of agonising self-control, but he gave way and blurted out the order. 'Take off your tunic and lie on the bed.'

Ann stood rigid. 'And why must I do that? Downstairs, they say you just want to stick your finger in every woman's quim, in the hope you find a virgin. Well, now you know that I am a virgin. There's no need to go on doing it.'

For a moment or so, the doctor stood trembling and beads of sweat stung his eyes. He stood as if something inside him was winding up, tightening some inside spring for action. Suddenly, as if his whole being was threatened, the spring snapped and he exploded, spun round on the spot, crashed forward against her and gripped her shoulders.

Ann tried to move backwards. But the bed blocked her retreat. For a moment, she felt a sickening fear. She felt the hot rage in the man —

felt the power of his hands and felt her body being flung sideways and sprawled over the bed. She tried to sit up, to wriggle free.

He released her left shoulder and with all his strength, swung his right arm and smashed his hand across her face. She didn't remember the hit or the falling back. All she was aware of was the spinning in her head and then the violent shaking of her head as he gripped handfuls of her hair. She opened her eyes to see the blur of his angry face.

He had leaned over her so that their noses almost touched. He was shouting, 'Now what do you say? What do you say now, convict?'

Ann groaned with pain, trying to think of something to say. 'I can't help meself,' she said, trying not to fumble the words. Slowly she remembered the advice of the Irish woman. 'I am here with you, doctor, and with God looking down on you. And God is very angry with both of us.'

'How do you know that?'

'Because He knows everything.'

The doctor stared into her face, as if looking for some sign. Nothing came and he shook himself like a dog trying to get rid of some itch. He trembled for a few moments then seemed to gather himself into control and stood back.

'You are right. Sometimes I feel God testing me. The Devil sits over my left shoulder and gives me feelings that I cannot control. It is not me, but the evil power that tries to rule me. But you, you don't help. I pray that I might be able to help you. But you are so vulgar, and so challenging, that the sick side of me boils to the surface. What can I do?'

'You could teach me to read and write. I know cooking and sewing. I know all them things. But I want to know how to read the word of God.'

Doctor Hall stood staring into her face as if looking for a truth. He ground his teeth and moved his lips about struggling to find words for someone as ignorant as this convict girl, who was not only beautiful, but a virgin. He nodded to himself, knowing that they both knew the meaning of the word virgin. In his experience, virginity was something rare. In the whole ship of some 108 women convicts, he had discovered only two virgins. He must choose one, at least. Months at sea with two untouched women close at hand was more than his nature could control. He stirred himself to talk.

'Certainly I could teach you the art of reading. It will take much longer for you to learn the physical art of writing. But first let me get to know you more. I can't help someone who doesn't trust me.'

Ann looked at him, listened to him as if she wanted to believe him. But her face stung and the doctor began to sound a bit too much, like the butler.

'Sorry, doctor, but I can't trust no teapot.'

'It's a pity someone hadn't taught you to speak properly. Or at least use manners. You will have to trust me. I am your doctor and I could be your friend. You are guilty of no crime, but here you are a convict because you didn't have a friend. You will need a friendly employer in Botany Bay. That is your only hope of some sort of happy life out there. I can see you are capable of education and responsive to prayer. You should stay here in the sickbay for a few days. I could settle your stomach problem and then perhaps we could start learning to read. I say this as a possible friend and as someone who actually admires your spirit.'

'I've heard girls call it lots of things, but I don't want no fingers digging into me spirit.'

He ignored her remark, but went on, 'Then we are in agreement.'

'I don't understand any agreements. The butler wanted an agreement. But I think I understand your big worry. So let's start proper like. Send me back to the cells and tomorrow if I'm sick again, you can bring me up here and we can talk. We can talk about God. We can talk about God and all his angels, but only so long as we don't touch and we can learn to read bits from the Bible. And you can tell me why it is that God lets innocent people suffer because teapots tell lies and do filthy things.'

Doctor Hall tried to look friendly. He tried to sound like a friend and he babbled on about his hopes to settle in Botany Bay, or Sydney and to start a new life. Perhaps even raise a family. He gave Ann an occasional pat on the shoulder, but whenever he moved closer to her, Ann reminded him of his love of God. This play went on for more than one hour without any results. By then he gave up, called the sickbay sailor with a tap on the table, and Ann was taken back to the cells.

Down there, surrounded by the crowd of smelly women, she sank into her hammock and almost smiled. She hadn't been poked or prodded as the women had warned. She'd been knuckled, but she'd kept her tunic on. Ann had survived her day and she had only five more months to survive.

4

The Irish Solution

Days and nights, whichever were which, dribbled past like water from a leaking tap. And, save for such things as the foul food, the forever overflowing slop bucket, sailors seeking the lower half of any available convict, the entire ship sweltered under the all suffusing smell of increasingly frail women who had long lost sight of any future and whose only relief was to fall in and out of friendships. There was little else. But all the while the *Mary Anne* lolled and rolled into warmer, bluer skies and ocean.

The tub bathing on deck was abandoned and the women were allowed on deck to take sun and wash with buckets of seawater. The women enjoyed the sun and the sailors enjoyed their daily entertainment. The bosun even tired of hitting women with his length of rope. He made unsuccessful attempt to have sex with convicts, but eventually gave up and simply got on with the business of driving the sailors up and down the rigging and forever having the men adjust sails.

Ann stayed entire, despite regular trips to the sick bay and the sweaty attention of Doctor Hall. Others weren't so lucky.

Doctor Hall discovered a young girl who everyone called Sally, though she kept her real name to herself. Sally had been a serving girl in London and was caught red-handed with her apron full of silver cutlery. Apparently, she planned to cash in the silver and head to Scotland. Everyone said that Sally was attractive. At something less than fifteen years old, she was short and slim with long ginger hair. Her outstanding factor in life was her ability to read and write. This kept her busy taking dictation and writing down letters for other convicts in their hope the letters could be posted, though they were more likely to be sent back on the return voyage of the *Mary Anne*.

Doctor Hall, who twirled his fingers in and out, soon discovered her physical state of being. Her hymen was intact. Delighted, he shifted his attention from Ann. He congratulated Sally on her condition and wished her well in the future. For him, it was not to end. From his day of discovery, he kept her supplied with small treats, better food and the promise of a good life in New South Wales. He also promised her his faithfulness in the years to come. His only problem was Sally's aversion to losing her virginity. He tried reasoning – to no avail. She told him she would rather die first and she would maintain her virginity until the night she was formally married.

Doctor Hall faced his challenge with a sense of certainty. He was certain that with a bit of gentle massage in the right area, supported by better food, he would succeed. Besides, he had four months to work on it.

He lost the competition, long before the next month was up. Sally won and it was Irish who engineered Sally's rescue.

Sally's sixth visit to the sickbay was much longer than usual. She simply lay back and waited for the usual probing examination. Doctor Hall looked at her bemused. She seemed to anticipate his moves with a controlled excitement.

Down in the cells, the women waited, knowing what faced Sally, but not understanding her acceptance of her situation. However, the suspicion that Sally was about to be deflowered by the doctor was not shared by Irish. She simply sat in the gloom with her back to the ship's side and played melancholy Scottish tunes on the tin whistle.

Eventually, Sally was dragged back, barely conscious. The two sickbay sailors opened the cell door and flung the girl to the floor like a broken puppet. She was quietly weeping and shaking. Blood was smeared across her face. Two of the women nursed Sally into a sitting position while one wiped her face clean.

'What the Hell happened?' several woman asked at once.

'They tried to kill me, that's what. They knuckled me all over, kicked me all around the ship, swore at me and hit me as hard as they liked.'

'You didn't hit back?'

'How could I? I just wanted to keep me teeth in me head as best I could. One of them ripped me tunic off me and they took turns to flog me with a length of wet canvas. I'm not going to make it to Botany Bay. If this is how I'm going to be looked after, I'd rather die first.'

Ann couldn't understand what had brought on the bashing. 'What did you do?' she asked.

'Nothing much. But I knew I had to trick the doctor somehow. He was forever sticking his finger into me. He said he had to make sure I was still really a virgin. But this time was different. He had the two sailors hold me down while he stuck his finger inside. Well, this time he gets a real shock. I wasn't a virgin any more. There was nothing there to block his finger. He all but exploded. Like a cannon, he did. Then, he just stood back and swung a haymaker, smashed me in the face, knocked me head over turkey off the bed and onto the floor. Nearly knocked me into next week. Then he shouted at me, right in me face, screaming about who had done it. He was sure some sailor had had his way for a couple of biscuits. I didn't say nothing. So he had the sailors chuck me back on the bed again and he said over and over again that I was a fool. He was certain that I had ruined his life and all that. I thought he was going to cry. He said that as long as I was a virgin we was safe. He wanted to be the only one to make me a woman, proper like. He kept mumbling that he would have done a good job looking after me in Botany Bay and we was going to be together for the rest of me life.'

Ann wasn't sure what to do. Or even if she could do anything at all. She lifted Sally onto her feet and the two walked over to Ann's bed. 'Tell me how it started,' she asked.

'I couldn't see any way out. We is trapped here on this ship and he's got everything he wants. I had to solve me problem. I was just sore all the time from his mucking about with me. Besides, I knew that in the end he'd win. Sometimes he would use two and three fingers at the same time and I wouldn't know what was happening. Sometimes, I wasn't sure if he was using his fingers or his spout. I just didn't know what to do. So I got help.'

'What sort of help?'

'Well, I tried to do it myself. But every time I touched meself down there, I was haunted by me mother. She told me that girls who touch themselves like that go blind and after a while they die and go straight to Hell.'

'It was me,' Irish said. She'd stopped playing and joined Sally and Ann. 'I could see the girl would have no chance. In the end, she'd be raped whenever the doctor needed to offload a bellyful. So we did a short cut.'

Ann couldn't understand. 'What sort of short cut?'

Sally covered her face with both hands and started to sob. 'Irish helped me. She told me to lie down with me knees up and open. Then she took her tin whistle. She didn't bother with the part she blows in, but she wrapped the bottom half in a bit of clean petticoat and gently pushed it inside me. Well, first she used two fingers to sort of hold me open and then slipped the whistle in. As soon as she came up against something inside, she just jabbed until the stuff inside tore. It didn't hurt much, but there was a lot of blood and we had a load of trouble to clean it all up.

Ann was numb. 'It must have hurt.'

'Not much. It was the punch-up from the doctor and the two sailors that hurt most. I don't want to go through that again,'

'She'll be tops now,' said Irish with a laugh. 'That so-called doctor won't worry her from now on. And besides, Sally will forever have a love of good music. Well, Irish music anyway. She'll have to write in her diary thing that on this day, in the cause of high-art music, she was deflowered by an Irish whistle.'

'But the doctor shouted at me, wanting to know what sailor I been with. I couldn't tell about the tin whistle, so I told him there was just too many sailors to count. I said all the sailors loved me and they was queued up all over the deck. The doctor screamed at me and ordered me out. Then, them two sickbay sailors dragged me out for a good hiding. The doctor was sure it was one of them was the culprit. He swore at them and threated they'd never see Botany Bay alive.'

'Well, it's all over now,' repeated Irish.

'I hope so. What'll happen if I ever get married? Will he know?'

'Not if you're nice to him at the time. But if it gets to be a real worry, just tell the lucky man the truth.' Irish thought it was a good joke against the doctor and offered her services to Ann.

Ann tried to see herself being deflowered by an Irish tin whistle. She couldn't face it. But it was at that moment she determined to fight for her virginity until she was ready, and wanting to arrange all that messy business with a man she liked enough to spend her life with. She didn't want some creepy teapot hanging around looking for somewhere to push his spout. The image of the butler flooded her head. It was a flooding that left a shudder throughout her body. But now there were two teapots. The butler and the doctor, they were both that sort of teapot, both of them only thinking of their drippy little spouts. What useless creatures they both were; one back in England, the other one working himself up to make trouble in Botany Bay.

'My trouble now is I don't have someone I can trust,'she whispered to herself. 'Why didn't my mother give me more warnings about what men wanted?' Ann recalled snippets of conversation with her mother when her first period started. Her mother had said very quietly that some men do dreadful things; things she could only hint at. But she hadn't raised the question of anything about using something like a tin whistle as a sort of protection.

Ann looked at Sally with affection, even though she couldn't be with her in her fight against Doctor Hall. But Doctor Hall also held her secret ambition. Between Sally and Doctor Hall, she would learn to write. She would put her life down on bits of paper and she would make the guilty ones suffer when her story was read and talked about.

5

Rio de Janeiro

Everyone, with the exception of 108 female convicts, declared Rio de Janeiro to be a wonderful port of call.

That night, their first in Rio, the trio of Ann, Irish and Sally sat together in the putrid gloom of the cells, laughing as they heard the sailors rowing back to the rhythm of bawdy songs. The women were hungry, but that night there was no food. Not even salt pork and rotten biscuits. Apparently, the cooks had gone ashore. All but three of them had returned, but were by then so drunk they could neither cook nor stand.

The next morning, eight bells rang out the time for the flogging of four men capable of standing and sober enough to understand their surroundings. After that, the women were allowed on deck to wash and to see the city across the bay. The buildings were almost hidden among palm trees and a few women who said they knew how to swim wondered if they could slip over the side and swim to the docks. One of the sailors had told them that the brothels in Rio were lavish, with gold platters and buckets of free food. It was also claimed that the women earned a fortune and within two years of working the night shift in Rio, they could return to England as respectable ladies, buy a big house in London and never work again. Apparently, light-skinned girls were rare and in demand.

The conversations didn't last long, as another woman told all that the waters were alive with hungry sharks. She went on to explain that being fed to the sharks was the standard form of capital punishment. Apart from understanding how she would like to see the butler fed into a seething, feeding-frenzy of huge sharks, Ann couldn't understand how anyone could bring themselves to actually throw a man or woman to such a terrible death. She knew she would be unable to do it. She would love to see the butler screaming for mercy and she would torture him more by telling him that the sharks wouldn't eat him in one go, but take small bites starting with his feet and working up until there was only his screaming head left. Then in one gulp the butler would be gone forever. As the daydream ended, it left her with an overwhelming sensation of the exquisite pleasure of revenge.

As to the rest of the conversation, Ann couldn't believe that prostitutes could return from Rio as well dressed, rich women. She remembered the assurance that Botany Bay would be a sort of Paradise, only five days from England and just off the south coast of France. The south of France was a bit of gossip that proved untrue, months ago. No one talked about it any more. She was sure all the gossip about Rio would prove the same.

However, all was not black. The convict women's first breakfast in Rio was different. Each convict received the usual ration of salt pork, biscuits, a slice of roast beef, a sludge of peas, and an orange. It was the orange that confused and delighted everyone. The orange turned breakfast into a party. Each one was as round as a cricket ball, yellow, and put out a perfume with the power to sweep out the scent of the slop bucket. The women rolled the fruit around in their hands, squeezed gently and endlessly sniffed the skin. They all knew what an orange was; most had seen such fruits in London. But for most it was their first touch of one. So taken were they by the colour and the heady aroma, the women were reluctant to bite into the skin to get at the juicy part inside.

Ann revelled in the orange. Her mouth tingled with the juice and it tickled her throat. She would never forget that breakfast. She had never before known such a sensuous pleasure as she enjoyed that morning. She didn't want to swallow her first bite, but to hold her mouth full of juicy orange that thrilled her senses and lifted her dreams of a better life with wonderful things to come.

6

Forever Onward

After Rio and the last of the oranges, there was no talk of the women escaping to earn huge fortunes and returning to England in bejewelled glory. There was nothing, but the cell-dark, ship-bucketing, slosh-spilling and seasick monotony of a never ending, seemingly pointless ship-rocking. Ann believed in the pit of her being that the journey would never end; that there would be no more ports till the end of time. But she was wrong. Although the days turned into fortnights, the *Mary Anne* did stop, if only for a handful of days.

That first dark morning, Ann woke to happy shouting on deck and an uneasy sense of going nowhere. The ship had stopped, but lolled about, rolling gently from side to side, and it wasn't long before a sailor came down to tell the women that they had safely docked in the Cape. As he left, he shouted that there would be no breakfast, but with a bit of luck, better food would be bought in the Cape, and within a couple of days they'd all be as fat as pigs.

'I'm sure you're right,' said Ann to herself. 'And Botany Bay is just off the coast of France and we'll have better food than we ever knew possible.'

Irish chuckled to Ann. 'I think we've heard all that before. But an orange would be nice.'

A few minutes later, the women were ordered up on deck for washing. On deck, the sun was well up and it lit a harbour crowded with ships of all shapes and sizes.

Irish pointed out a small boat with a triangular sail. 'I think that's an Arab boat. They say they trade, all up and down from here to India.'

'We going to India?' Ann asked her.

'Hope not. They reckon India is a pretty place, but it's a long way from Botany Bay.'

Sailors were lowering two rowing boats and scudding off across the bay. Ann looked past the collection of buildings along the shore to the huge mountain rearing above the harbour. It was flat on top and she wondered how they had taken all the pointy parts off. '

'It's called Table Mountain,' said Irish. 'They say it's sacred to some of the people who live here.'

'What do they do?'

'Who?'

'The people who live there.'

'Probably the same as everyone else, wherever. They've got nice warm weather, so they probably grow things.'

'I hope they grow oranges.'

They both laughed and grabbed a bucket for an all-over wash. The seawater was cooler than Rio, but warmer than when the *Mary Anne* left England.

'It'll be seven years before I ever see England again. But just the same, I think I've had more baths on this ship than I had all my life in Norfolk.'

'If you're unlucky.

'Irish, why unlucky?'

'Well, do you really want to go back there? Have to live in all that trouble again. All that dirt. All them gentry folk hating anyone who isn't gentry. I think we might take Botany Bay by storm. See if we can get away from all that church stuff. Sing a few songs. Work up a bit of business. That's what we'll do, Ann Rumsby.'

The two would have talked all day in the sunshine, but the bosun ordered all the women below and he stood on the gunwale to welcome a boat full of produce from the Cape.

Two hours later, down in the dark, a sailor ordered a few of the convicts to the galley for rations. They left and everyone sat waiting – hoping for an orange.

They weren't disappointed. The girls arrived back laden with food. There was the usual salt pork and pease pudding. But this time, each convict was given two oranges, a large apple, a small loaf of bread and fresh water. Another girl returned with two buckets of fresh water for the women to wash the salt from their faces. None of the women could believe the difference the water made. They were glad of the sea water for their bodies, but the salt dried on their faces and, no matter how much they rubbed with cloth, the salt was pitted into the skin and seemed to shrink and stiffen their faces. Two cupped handfuls of fresh water and they felt human again. Irish played a few tunes and the women sang with gusto.

For five days or so, the *Mary Anne* lolled about in the Cape of Good Hope. For five days, the women convicts ate boiled potatoes, oranges, apples, fresh beef, good biscuits and a strange, lumpy red vegetable like potato.

No one knew what day it was, but whatever it was, a strong cold wind blew up from the south and the *Mary Anne* leaned against the wind, unfurled her sails and slowly wallowed out in the roads of the Cape and into the grey of the ocean. A sailor said that the next stop would be Van Diemen's Land. This put an element of fear into the women, as virtually none of them spoke Dutch. Forty-five were to be offloaded and all of them were certain that within a few days they would be fed to the pigs.

The next day, Doctor Hall had Ann returned to the sick bay, where she kept him at arm's length with a pleading to learn reading. He preferred a physical examination, but she soon had him opening the Bible and reciting the words of the Lord's Prayer. She could write the words 'Our Father who' in huge letters scrawled to cover the entire piece of paper.

'When we get to Botany Bay, I will get you a slate and you can copy out whole lines, over and over, until you are good at it.'

'Thank you, doctor. When I can write out all the words I know, proper like, I'll even know how to write me own name.'

'I will even know how to write *my* own name.' the doctor corrected. 'In Botany Bay, you will learn many things and I will be there to help you all the way. You can live virtually as a free woman in my house and we will be able to arrange your whole life.' He eased closer to her, trying to smell her hair as if it pleased him. 'You'll have soap and perfumes and your hair will shine in the sunlight. Ann, you are a strangely beautiful young woman, and together we can try to create adventure.'

Ann's problem was that she understood his use of the word adventure. And she was certain that such an adventure would lead to nothing but misery in the years ahead. Her mother had repeatedly warned her of such adventures. But Ann also knew that understanding something and acting on advice can be two different things. She wanted to know what such an adventure would feel like – down there. And how often she would like it. She knew it must bring excitement, but certainly it would eventually bring babies and, in consequence of that, grinding poverty.

'You make life sound so lovely,' she said softly.

'We can make it lovely,' he replied and his voice carried a ring of victory.

Ann considered his answer for only a moment or so. 'We'll have to wait and see what happens when we leave the *Mary Anne*,' she replied, trying to sound distant.

'Why wait? Let us start the adventure now.'

'Not till I can write out the words from the Bible. And besides, how will things be better when we get to Botany Bay?'

'Because I have influence. That's how.'

'What's it mean, influence?'

'I have a letter to deliver to the most important man in Parramatta. He runs everything and he is a man of God.'

'Has he got wandering hands like another man of God?'

'He most certainly does not. But he is in a position to assign convicts as servants and, if you can control your bad temper, he will assign you to work for me. But first we must be on level terms.'

'Then let's level all that in Botany Bay.'

The doctor simply shook his head and tried to take deep breaths. 'Ann,' he said as if pleading, 'I want you to think of me as a friend.

'Do friends go round sticking their fingers where they aren't wanted?'

'Ann, for the love of gentle Jesus, I am your surgeon. I want to protect you, look after you. Keep you out of harm's way.'

'That's good. I was frightened you would say you wanted to be like a brother to me.'

'Why brother?'

'Well, that's what the sailors say. They must come from funny families.

'Well, I am not in any way your brother. I have to confess before God that I just can't resist the excitement of being with you. The moment I am next to you, I want us to be together – forever.'

'Well, I don't feel the same way. I'm frightened of you. You want to have your way with me because I'm a virgin, and after that, I'll be chucked away like an old boot.'

'I promise before God that I will be your friend and protector as long as we both shall live.'

'I would like to believe you, but I can't.'

The doctor gave up, rapped on the table and had the two sailors take her back to the cells.

By the afternoon, the weather turned cold and squalls ripped at the sails. The ship was in trouble throughout the day and by nightfall the struggle between the *Mary Anne* and the combined wind and ocean worsened. The ship dived, reared and thrashed against the smashing and winding sea. Giant waves smashed across the upper decks. Many of the convicts were sick and the stench of vomit from the overflowing slop bucket, cobwebbed the air. No sailor came to empty the bucket so two girls tried to move it towards the steps to the deck above. It was hopeless. Besides,all the hatches were bolted shut and everyone realised that if the ship were to founder, none of the convicts would survive drowning. The lucky convicts had hammocks, which bucked about like a wild animal making the women throw up with nowhere to vomit except where they lay. Most had given up on screaming for help. No one came and those who were not sick whipped about in their hammocks and tried not to think of Heaven and Hell.

But that night was the worst recurring savagery of a living nightmare. Ann didn't know if it was night or day. With all the hatches shut down and no lights, she lay clinging to the edges of her hammock with both hands crossed over her chest. She wanted to cry for her mother. She managed not to be sick, but the girl in the next hammock threwup into the air above her and the spray blew across Ann's face and hands. She tried to wipe it off, but there was only the stiff canvas of her hammock. She wondered if she could stand, but recoiled knowing she would be ankle-deep in human soup. The soup was diluted by the slosh of seawater pouring in around the hatches. The ship reared, plungerolled and shuddered in the storm and, above the roar, she could hear rats squealing and drowning in the swill beneath her.

However, all that was just the beginning. The confusion seemed to last forever. But then, just as suddenly as the storm had erupted, there was calm. There were no sounds of life on the decks above. They hadn't heard any bells and many wondered if all the ship's crew had been washed into the sea and drowned. 'What if we're the only ones left? And if we ever get out of the cells, who will steer the ship?'

There was no more talk of sailing the ship. Women simply groaned in disbelief that the storm was over. They lay quietly trying to believe they were safe. Irish called to her. Ann knew it was Irish, but couldn't understand what was said. One of the women had a long-handled scrubber and she tried to sweep the slush from the cell into the passageway. The smell made her throw up again. No one moved. No one tried to stand or even sit astride the hammock.

'Thank God that's over,' one woman said quietly. But she spoke too soon.

There came a new and higher-pitched scream of wind, lashing into the *Mary Anne*. It seemed to come softly at first, but down there in the dark, no one knew the ship had passed through the eye of the storm. The gentleness didn't last. The roaring wind wound up and the women felt the ship lift her bows up and out of the ocean. The ship lifted until it seemed vertical, but only to collapse back on her rudder, as if to slide down through the waves to the very bed of the ocean never to be seen again. But she didn't. She tottered about as women clung to their hammocks, or slid along the deck, their arms and legs tangling with the other convicts.

Then, as if on some order, the *Mary Anne* bellyflopped forward and bashed herself down onto the surface of the sea. The crash was so strong it seemed that the ship must break apart. Many of the women were flicked from their hammocks as the storm screamed stronger. Women tried to clamber back onto their hammocks, without success. The ship spun, reared and rolled – all three at once – and the storm laughed at anyone who thought they could be saved. Many prayed to God and St Jude. Ann was bucked from her hammock and she slid about in the ankle-deep slosh on the deck, trying to cling to anything within reach.

Again and again, the *Mary Anne* rose and fell, and again and again the women gave up screaming and surrendered to nascent fear. Ann knew she was screaming, but in the overflowing shrieking and roaring, she couldn't hear her own voice. Nor could she see the palm of her hand even pressed flat against her nose.

But after four hours or so, the storm eased to nothing more than a zephyr, barely rippling the sails. Ann's body began to relax. She managed to grapple her way into her hammock. She lay and waited in the quiet for the last moments of the *Mary Anne*. She hoped she might die in her sleep. But she knew there would be no sleep. She knew the foul weather would start again and last all the way to Botany Bay. By then, most of the convict women would be either dead or their limbs all bent and broken. She imagined the sight of the sailors, if there were any of them left, throwing the women's mangled bodies into the sea before they reached Van Diemen's Land. She thought of her past life. She saw her soldier boy in their park. She brought up pictures of the butler and then Doctor Hall. In her mind, she could see the doctor and felt his hands moving all over her body. Strangely, he was gentle and she felt sorry for being so rough with him. But just as suddenly he was gone.

So was the storm. All around her was silence. She had been asleep, dreaming. She heard the sound of eight bells and she looked around to see how many women were still alive. She made out Irish and Sally and felt tears of relief. No one she knew had died.

7

Port Jackson

Ann stood on deck with her group, all of them shivering. They'd washed from buckets of salt water and scanned the vast expanse of a huge and seemingly empty harbour. She didn't wash much. The wind was colder than the water and she hoped the sun might suddenly shine and dry her skin. 'The month of May at home was always sunny and warm. Why isn't it like that now?'

She looked around, amazed that Port Jackson was so big. To her, it didn't look like a harbour, but just another ocean. She looked at the land and even close-by the wharf there were huge, spidery-looking trees from all the hills down to the rocks at the edge of the water. Looking back to the ocean, she focused on the two massive cliffs on either head. Then, looking up the harbour again, there was water as far as she could see. Nearby, there were islands and sandy beaches, more cliffs and mountains. Here and there, a few small buildings dotted the shoreline. The scene was overcast and cold. Nothing seemed friendly. Rowing boats eased the *Mary Anne* to the side of a rough wharf. Even the nearby buildings looked unfriendly and at the far edge of the wharf a handful of naked black people stood there looking -on. No one seemed to take any notice of them and Ann wondered if they were dangerous. She had heard of American Indians who had eaten white people. Nothing looked attractive or inviting.

'Why did we come all this way, cooped up in a filthy *Mary Anne*, bruised and battered by dreadful storms – just to find this? Why didn't we stop in some lovely, warm place like Rio?'

Irish stood beside her talking. 'It certainly isn't Rio or the south of

France, but I think it'll do,' she said nodding. 'There's sure to be a pub, that's the main thing. And we're a long way from the Old Bailey and all them slimy silvertails. And come what may, Annie, this place is going to need us. One of the Irish sailors, he's after having told me that there's not enough women to go around. So play your cards right, Annie, and we'll be able to do deals. That's for sure, for sure. And if you have to go into double harness, don't worry too much. If you have to get married, it don't have to be forever.'

She was interrupted by the bosun ordering the women to go below and bundle their bits and pieces to take ashore. He had no need to hurry. Three days later on 23 May, 1822, the convict women disembarked the *Mary Anne* and stood about on the quay looking lost.

For Ann, leaving the *Mary Anne* brought a new confusion. She had come to know the ship as an unfriendly, stinking, but manageable home. She was glad to be out of it and into daylight, but this was worse and everything was strange.

The wharf bustled with activity. Strings of convict men worked like donkeys carrying bundles from the ship. They rolled barrels down narrow gangplanks and steered rope slings loaded with big barrels and boxes from the ship's hold to the wharf. From the wharf, the men loaded everything onto carts. More convict men in heavy jackets against the cold, hauled the carts like oxen. Soldiers in untidy uniforms shouted commands and pushed the convicts about, designating bundles to be sorted into various heaps. There were rugged-up officials everywhere.

The doctor stood on the wharf, in his naval uniform, talking to officials about the health of the women convicts. He pretended not to see Ann and that gave her a few moments of relief. But it wasn't long before the women were given orders to pick-up and start walking.

Ann was unsteady, trying to adjust her legs and balance to solid ground again and hearing rude and even a few friendly calls from men who had arrived to look for possible wives and workers. Ann looked them over. They wore rough clothes to start with. They were obviously not convicts. Convicts wore distinctive jackets. These men were not dressed like officers or English gentlemen. Some were grubby, in need of a shave, and many looked hungry. Several came close enough to give her and the other girls a good looking over. They seemed to agree that the girls who had strong-looking arms and big bosoms were the best to take home.

'Show us your legs,' one man shouted.

Ann wondered if the men would want to look at their teeth as well. The men followed the girls along the wharf to get a better view from different angles.

Ann knew she was picked out by one man who shouted, 'I bags the one with frizzy hair. She looks like she can fight.'

Ann pretended not to hear.

The girls walked no more than a hundred yards when they were stopped. A soldier read out names and those called, including Ann Rumsby, were herded into a smaller group.

Irish was with a second group. She shouted something to Ann, but another soldier threatened her to be silent. 'I think he's English, poor sod,' she started to say, but didn't get any more out before the soldier threatened her with the butt of his musket.

A man in rough clothes shouted to the soldier not to 'damage dacent Irish goods!' It sounded like a warning.

'And what'll you do about it, Paddy?' shouted back the soldier.

'Nothing much, I'll just break your bloody English neck, that's all.'

'We're off to a great start,' murmured Ann, and the girl next to her said it would be best to keep mum till they knew the lie of the land.

Ann nodded and whispered, 'Lie of the land is all right. But I just hope I never have to go anywhere, ever again, by boat.'

8

The Third Trial

For Ann, not only the trees but even the houses were different. The front of the Douglass house was odd. The door yawned wide open and swung outside so that anyone could, more or less, see in. Well, almost – the doorway was half-hidden by a makeshift curtain of plaited strips of jute.

Ann shook her head. 'Strange people,' she muttered, 'They know they is surrounded by wild-looking blacks to say nothing of mobs of light-fingered convicts, but they leaves their front door wide open.'

She knocked on the wall beside the doorway and stood back. A woman's friendly voice shouted for her to enter. She carefully parted a few of the jute strips and stepped in. It was a darkened room with no rugs on the floor and the walls were bare. A rough-looking dresser stood against the dark wall while an elegant woman in a long dress with its collar high up on her throat sat on the opposite side of the room be-tween the small windows and a very small table. The middle of the room was dominated by a long table surrounded by an odd assortment of chairs. The woman was sewing with a mess of green cloth that over-flowed her lap onto the wooden floor.

The woman looked up and in a commanding voice asked, 'And who, may I ask, are you? And perhaps more importantly, what are you doing here?'

She had the tone of a boss, but Ann liked the lilt in her voice. The woman spoke with a soft Irish accent that was friendly – a bit like Irish from the ship, but this one had a very classy sound. Ann hoped the woman herself would be friendly. If such were the case, the change would be lovely.

'I'm from the Factory, m'am,' she said quietly – trying to sound servile. 'Doctor Douglass is the master there and he told me to come here.'

'And why did he do that?'

'He asked me what I did in England and when I told him what I was in service like, he told me to come here and help you. I hope that's all right, m'am.'

'Then do you know who I am?' the woman asked quietly.

'I think so, m'am.'

'Then who do you think I am?'

'I think you is the wife of Doctor Douglass.'

'Yes. I am Mrs Douglass.'

'Then I am glad to be here, m'am.'

'Then I am glad to be here, Mrs Douglass,' the woman corrected.

'Yes m'am.'

'Yes, Mrs Douglass!'

'Yes, Mrs Douglass,' Ann repeated.

'Then tell me before we get started, why are you here?'

'Because Doctor Douglass sent me.' She started to mouth 'm'am', but swallowed the word and hurried out 'Mrs Douglass' instead.

'Good. You are a fast learner. But what I need to know is why you are not in England, instead of this God-forsaken Parramatta?'

'Because they told lies about me in Norfolk.'

'I'm sure they did, whoever they were, but what sort of lies?'

'Well, they said I was a whore.'

'And of course you were no such thing. Am I right?'

'Yes, Mrs Douglass. I was never a whore. I am a virgin. I never been with nobody. Well, not like that anyway.'

'Of course not.'

Ann could see she was not believed and blushed. Suddenly she felt herself a small girl again, confronted by an in-charge adult. She rolled her right ankle as if doing something might just solve the problem. 'I don't mind that people don't believe me,' she said, 'but I got proof that I am a virgin, Mrs Douglass,' she blurted out.

Mrs Douglass looked Ann over as she might have inspected a prospective horse.

'Well, I must say. That is very clever of you to get proof. So you've never been married? Not even on a casual, shall we say one-night basis, or even now and again perhaps?'

'Certainly not, Mrs Douglass.'

'And of course you've never been pregnant? Not even a little bit?'

'How could I?'

'Well, I am sure you could if you tried. Most Parramatta girls don't find that event difficult. And I must say that girls here, in Parramatta, find it comes to them remarkably easily, if not miraculously. Many have sworn to virgin births. However, I am intrigued. How did you come by this proof?'

'From Doctor Hall on the ship *Mary Ann*.'

Mrs Douglass suddenly stiffened at the name Hall. 'And he gave you proof?'

'Yes, Mrs Douglass.'

'Well, now. I'm not only intrigued, but apprehensive. How did this Doctor Hall produce such proof?'

'From tests.'

'What tests precisely?'

'Tests with his fingers, Mrs Douglass.'

'Ye gods, girl, where?'

Ann scrambled for thoughts, not knowing a safe answer. 'From the ship, *Mary Anne*.'

'Let's stop this inquisition for a moment, girl. What is your name?'

'Ann, Mrs Douglass.'

'Ann what?'

'Ann Rumsby.'

Mrs Douglass suddenly relaxed. For a few moments, she breathed heavily, looking down at her sewing. She soon stopped, pushed the needle into a fold in the cloth as if for safe keeping and looked up. She spoke as if she felt reluctant to continue the conversation. 'Ann

Rumsby,' she said slowly, 'please feel easy, but tell me about these tests by our well known Doctor Hall.

'They was done on the ship. He tested every girl on the ship.'

Mrs Douglass looked at Ann with a flash of anger. 'For the love of Mary, where were the tests conducted?'

'In the doctor's sickbay.'

'I can see that this is going to take longer than the journey from England to Port Jackson. Tell me for the last time: were these tests performed on your body?'

'Yes, Mrs Douglass.'

'Where on your body?'

Ann rolled her ankle again and began to breathe heavily. She didn't want to answer. Instead, she closed her eyes and, with her finger, pointed down to the front of her hips.

'Can you be more precise? Do you have a name for that part of your body?'

Ann blurted out her answer. 'Down there,' she said, ashamed of having to admit such a thing.'

She heard Mrs Douglass suck in air and mutter Gaelic swear words – just the same as Irish did. Finally she said in English, 'Dear God and Hail Mary, Thou art full of grace.'

Ann opened her eyes to see what was happening around her.

Mrs Douglass sat stiff, her own eyes closed and shaking her head as if in disbelief of what she had heard. 'And what do you call that part of you?'

'It's me quim.'

'Dear God. Ann, please, whenever you are in this house, do not use vulgar language – especially that word.'

'But that's what they all say.'

'Well, not in this house they don't.'

'Well, what do I say?'

'The correct word is vagina.'

'I don't think I got one of them. Probably high-class ladies got one of them, but not a working girl like me anyway. We just got a quim.'

'The vagina is what every woman in the whole world has. It's the nothing-thing that causes us nothing but trouble. So what do you call it?'

Ann stumbled over the new word, 'Vag something.'

'Vagina. Now, say it again.'

'Vagina.'

'Good. Now tell me, how did Doctor Hall touch you there?'

'He had two sailors hold me down on the bunk and he pushed his finger inside me. He did it with all the girls.'

'What a pervert,' she murmured. 'And why did he do that?'

'Because he was looking to see if he could find a virgin.'

'And I suppose he was very nice to you after he found you were a virgin?'

'He promised to help me here in Parramatta.'

'More likely he promised to help himself in Parramatta. I'll wager he also promised that he would set you up in a house in Sydney and he talked of love and protection. Am I right?'

'Something like that, Mrs Douglass.'

'Tell me, Ann Rumsby, were there any other virgins discovered?'

'Only one, Mrs Douglass, a girl called Sally. She's a good girl and she knows the reading and writing.'

'And is this clever girl still a virgin?'

'I think so, Mrs Douglass. She tricked Doctor Hall.'

'She must have been clever to do that. What trick did she use?'

'She used the bottom end of a penny whistle. Well, she didn't. She was a bit frightened so she got Irish, another girl on the ship, who plays Irish music, to do it for her.'

'You mean to tell me that this Sally girl had an Irish musician push the end of the whistle into her vagina. Was there bleeding?'

'They both said so.'

'And this trick worked?'

'Yes, m'am, I mean, Mrs Douglass.'

'How did this trick confuse Doctor Hall?'

'Sally told him she had been with a couple of sailors – well, she said she'd been with lots of sailors. When he heard that, Doctor Hall he lost his temper and hit her so hard, we thought he'd smashed her jaw. She couldn't eat for two days. Then he had his two helpers take her out and they belted her black and blue just for good measure.'

'I hope that was the end of that trick?'

'Yes, Mrs Douglass. After the beating, Sally didn't have no more trouble. Doctor Hall just left her alone. Kept his sticky fingers to hisself.'

'But not from you?'

'No. He got worse. Wanted to test me every other day. They reckon he was just trying to work me up.'

'And you weren't tempted to try the Irish solution?'

'I kept it in the back of me mind. But I never did.'

'I'm surprised you lived through it all. How did you survive?'

'God helped me.'

'Well, that's a miracle. What did God say?'

'He didn't say nothing. He never does. In fact, I don't think God is there, or anywhere at all. Well, not for working girls anyway. But I told Doctor Hall that God was on my side and that God told me that the doctor should teach me to read the Bible.'

'And that worked?'

'Yes, Mrs Douglass.'

'I must say, I have never been so intrigued. How often did you produce this God-bothering trick of yours?'

'Every time he got pokey with his fingers.'

'For five months? You kept that obnoxious man at bay for the entire voyage?'

'Yes.'

'But he has affected you just the same.'

'Well, I am still a virgin, but I don't feel like one. I don't have anywhere on me that's just for me. Before him with his fingers, that part of me was a secret. I didn't share down there with no one. But now it's not a secret. It was lifted from me and I know I'll never be the same again.'

After a few more breathed-out Gaelic swear words, the older woman gathered herself and tried to sound aloof. 'Tell me, Ann Rumsby, do you think you could work in the same house with your Doctor Hall and keep what's left of your secret?'

'I couldn't. He'd have the rest of his way. He'd be sort of soft at first, but then he'd lose his temper and knock me silly.'

'And after that, he'd be out and about digging around for another virgin.'

'And I'd be out and about with a bellyful of arms and legs. A sort of single mother and a second-hand girl.'

This was followed by a few moments of more Gaelic and heavy breathing.

'Ann Rumsby,' she said firmly, but very quietly, 'I would be happy to have you in this house for a few days, but we needs be careful. It will take time for you to recover from all this. Let me explain what I think. And what I think is something strictly between you and me. Understood?'

'Yes, m'am.'

Both then spoke in unison, 'Yes, Mrs Douglass.'

'Ann, I want you to go back to the Factory, spend the night there and tomorrow morning you return here with any possessions you may have. Doctor Douglass will be here after his ride from Sydney. I will tell him everything you have told me. He will then arrange for you to stay in this house on a somewhat permanent basis. Later on, he will find you a suitable employer and we will look around for a convict, or free settler who will be a suitable husband. Do you think we could manage all that?'

'I will try, Mrs Douglass. But I don't want no husband. Well, not just now anyway.'

'Why not?'

'Well, Doctor Hall with his tests, he put me off. He had terrible fingernails and he scratched me inside. A husband might want to do that all the time.'

'Not a real husband, and certainly not with his fingers.'

'No. But I think the spout thing might be worse. I've seen that part on a few teapots and it don't look like anything good. It's sort of ugly and floppy. I don't want nothing to do with it.'

'Good. Keep it that way. But let me tell you that with the right man, things would be different. But more importantly, a husband can be an essential protector.'

'But he's still a teapot.'

'I'm sure he will be, but he can also be a reliable guard dog who will keep uninvited teapots outside the gate. Now, off you go, Ann Rumsby, and you return here tomorrow morning, after breakfast. Is that clear?'

'Yes, Mrs Douglass. I am very lucky to meet you.'

Ann left by the same open door and dawdled back to the Factory. It was just as well she did dawdle. She tried to enjoy the open air, even if the trees looked like skeletons. And it was cold. In the morning early, the ground had a covering of white frost. It disappeared with the sunrise but everything was wrong. At home, May was lovely, the cold was gone and the trees and bushes were sprouting green leaves and birds' nests. June would bring hot days and lovely nights.

Parramatta made its own punishments. Even for them that ran the place. On arrival, she was told that a Dr Hall and the Reverend Samuel Marsden had visited the Factory and had asked for Ann Rumsby. They had left, not knowing where she was. Apparently, Marsden was not happy to be involved in meeting a convict girl. His only interest was whether the convict Rumsby was Irish. Nor was he convinced when the convict women told him she was English and he went away muttering about the Devil, and all his works, that blossomed within the Irish nation.

9

The Fourth Trial

Mary Wooten had arrived in Sydney along with Ann Rumsby on the *Mary Anne*. She was lucky and only two days after her arrival in Parramatta's Female Factory she was assigned to the house of Doctor Douglass. In that house, where there were no real curtains, where the front door swung out, instead of in, and none of the furniture matched, there were several assigned servants, headed by a young man named Andrew White.

At the end of her first day, Mary was happy with her conditions and took a fancy to Andrew White. He was unmarried, good-looking and seemed gentle. Above all, he was looking for a wife. Apparently, Mrs Douglass had offered to help him find a suitable convict. Mary was happy. She was not frightened of the men that Ann Rumsby called teapots. In her short life, Mary had known many men. Doctor Hall had fingered out her lack of physical virginity and, despite her pretty face and happy personality, he ignored her. Mary said he had found two possible virgins in Ann and Sally.

Mary had seen Ann leave the Douglass house that afternoon and the next morning she worked around the living room and the kitchen in the hope that Ann might return.

When Ann did arrive, Mrs Douglass was not up and about. Ann walked into the big room and shuffled her feet on the floor. Mary heard the sound and rushed in. The two girls flung their arms around each other and almost cried with happiness to meet in a house of hope. Their reunion didn't last long. Andrew White entered and sent Mary off to concoct a mixture of wine and cough medicine for Mrs Douglass, who he said was feeling off-colour.

Andrew took his time to look Ann up and down. After a moment or so, he relaxed and smiled his approval. 'If you keep your head down in this house, you'll do well,' he told her, and quickly went on to explain that a certain Doctor James Hall had arrived earlier in the morning and asked for her.

'I don't want to see him.'

'You might have no choice in the matter, but why not?'

'Because he wants to do me harm, that's why.'

'That's what it costs for girls who want to get on. You married?'

'No. And I don't want no such a thing.'

'Well, a husband is probably your best bet against creeps like Doctor Hall. Get yourself married, have a man to look after you and treat you well. Could even give you a family, as a sort of extra package.'

'Thank you, Andrew White. Thanks for your advice. But I'm in no shape to get married and I want to feel settled first. I still feel sick from the ship.'

'You'll be all right. And besides, you look in pretty good shape to me.'

The inquisition might have gone on, but someone knocked on the front wall and Ann, expecting trouble, rushed off through the doorway taken by Mary Wooten. Mary was dusting shelves with a crumpled rag, but when they heard Andrew and another man talking together in the big room, Mary lifted her hand, signalling Ann to stay put and to keep quiet. Ann guessed what was happening and stood silent, feeling that everything her mother had warned her of was about to start happening. The thought of her mother, warm and cuddly, brought on a flush of tears.

The voices in the big room stopped and a moment later, Mary returned looking fearful.

'Andrew told Sticky Fingers you was busy, so the doctor said he'd come back in a while. I'm sorry, Annie, but you'll just have to face him.'

Ann Rumsby stood cold. The tears stopped running and anger swelled instead. 'I will face him now,' she said and walked through the house.

At the front door, there was no sign of Doctor Hall and she ran to the gate. From there, she saw him with another man walking down the road that everyone said led to Sydney. She started to run as if desperate to meet a new fate. She had run only a hundred yards or so when Doctor Hall heard her steps and turned. It was as if she were running like a lover, breathless and with tears streaking her face.

'My little Ann Rumsby,' he said softly to her and told the other man to continue on his journey.

Ann stopped still, looking around at the skinny trees on either side of the track. A third man was just ahead, standing by a gateway. The man at the gate pretended not to notice, but kept his face side-on while watching every move the couple made.

'Ann, I have good news for you,' Doctor Hall started. 'I have already found a suitable house and the Reverend Marsden is happy to organise your transfer. You will be my assigned servant in our new house. Your life will be starting as if there was never a past.'

Ann was uncomfortably aware of the gateman watching. She looked around for somewhere private so she could speak her mind. Anger swelled up in her, but she knew she must be careful. She had to avoid making an enemy. Doctor Hall was like the butler. He was a man of power. They were both frightening people and they could ruin your life.

While Ann stood mute, Doctor Hall gently grasped her elbow and led her into the bushy wattles beside the road. The gateman found that move more than interesting and it stirred feelings in him he hadn't had for some time. It was also a long time since he had been provided with any entertainment. He had to make several moves and finally, he needed to crouch low on his hands and knees in the middle of the road to keep the two of them in view.

Doctor Hall tried to embrace Ann and to kiss her on top of her head. She swivelled free, her eyes flashing with a fearful anger.

'Doctor Hall, I am happy where I am,' she blurted out. 'Mrs Douglass is good to me, but if I'm not careful the doctor and Mrs Douglass will be the ruin of me.'

'How so?'

'Well, they want to marry me off to another convict servant. And that is something I don't want.'

'Ann, I know you need me. You will always be special to me. But I have heard of this Doctor Douglass. He has the reputation of being a lecher. Has he touched you?'

'No. He hasn't and he won't come back until this afternoon. I'll see him then.'

'Then we must act quickly. I will return later today with the Reverend Marsden and we will solve your problem.'

'Doctor Hall, I don't want no one to solve no problem. I can solve all me own problems meself. And Mrs Douglass is kind to me.'

'Ann, listen carefully. I am your only true friend in this far-off place. You must also be careful of Mrs Douglass. You must surely be aware that she is Irish.'

'So what? Why do all you lot hate the Irish?'

'Because they are Catholic. They practise cannibalistic rituals and they are dangerous.'

'I know who's dangerous. It's people like you and the butler.'

'I am no danger to you, or anyone else for that matter. I simply want to protect you. Convert you into a Christian woman. I can make you happy and keep all the predators away.'

'You mean, keep all the teapots outside the fence?'

Doctor Hall tried again to embrace Ann, but she swivelled out of reach like a boxer. Eventually, she did surrender to one quick embrace which terminated in her bursting into a flood of tears.

The gateman, who Ann was to later know by the name of Scrummy Jack, practically fell on the road with excitement. No doubt he was hoping the couple would suddenly rip off their clothes and thrash about in frantic sex all over the clearing. He started wriggling forward on his hands and knees to get a better view. He achieved his plan, but was disappointed. He saw nothing more than Ann pull away and Doctor Hall push something into her pocket. He saw Doctor Hall move off, leaving

Ann in tears. Doctor Hall walked back to the road, past Scrummy Jack, who by then had spun onto his backside and seemed to be trying to repair his boot, all the while facing the other way. Hall hurried off down the track towards Sydney.

Ann waited alone for a few minutes, wiped tears from her face with the back of her hand and stumbled back onto the road. Scrummy Jack offered to look after her for the rest of the day. Ann recoiled in disgust, turned and ran as fast as she could, back to the house of Mrs Douglass.

Andrew White was waiting at the open front door when Ann burst through the open gateway and slowed to a jog. She brushed past him into the big room.

'Why the waterworks?' Andrew asked gently. Then he grinned, 'Did the dirty doctor try his hand again?'

'No. No worry. He just wants to cause trouble for me and Doctor Douglass.'

'I bet he gave you something to go on with.'

Ann fumbled in her pocket for a piece of paper. She pulled it out and at that moment Andrew gave a low whistle. Ann was holding a banknote. It was strange and covered in writing.

'Looks like you been bought for ten shillings. You're a sort of expensive slave girl.'

'Ten shillings? Is that what that bit of paper is worth? I never seen one before, not one like that.'

'I haven't seen one meself. But I know they's around. They come by ship from London. Before this, we only had the dollar and dump coins from the Cape.'

'Ten shillings. That teapot doctor thinks he can buy me for ten shillings.'

Andrew laughed and flapped the note in his hand. 'The thing is,' he said quietly, 'for ten shillings he could buy most of the whores in Parramatta. You've got yourself a protector there, Annie.'

'I got nothing of the sort. All I got is ten shillings and he's going to be hanging around wanting his money's worth.'

'Will you give the money back?'

'I should, but I won't. It'll be the biggest ten shillings he's ever lost.'

'That lost bit isn't a bad idea, Annie. Next time you sees him, tell him you lost his ten-shilling note and could he please get you another one.'

'I will not. And please keep all this to yourself.'

Ann didn't wait for any further advice and walked through the house looking for Mary Wooten.

10

The Fifth Trial

The next morning didn't bode well for the Douglass household. Matthew White was fussing about giving orders to Mary while Mrs Douglass ate breakfast with Doctor Douglass in the front room, filling the whole house with a strained silence. Doctor Douglass looked grim, but said nothing, as if quietly planning an unpleasant conversation. Ann kept out of the way. She dusted furniture in the next room. It was the first time that she actually took notice of the dust. She was surprised by the redness of it.

'Everything in this country is red,' she murmured. 'In Norfolk, dust is sort of dirty grey, but here it's red.' Yesterday, she noticed that even the new leaves on the tips of the strange-looking trees outside were red. She only knew leaves in Norfolk to be green. She kept working, dusting the books against the wall, but kept her eyes open and her hearing bent to the possible sounds of footsteps outside. Her stomach churned as she anticipated an unwelcome visit from Doctor Hall and his creepy fingers.

Mary Wooten removed the breakfast plates from the table and Doctor Douglass retired to his room to finish dressing. Mrs Douglass moved around the house as if keeping fit for a struggle to come. Ann knew she was the cause of the tension throughout the house and she wondered if Mrs Douglass had talked about Doctor Hall to her husband. She was frightened that perhaps Mrs Douglass and her husband had had an argument and Doctor Douglass might support Hall. 'Most teapots sit together,' she muttered and her head swum with fear that, between the two doctors, she would be packaged off to Sydney to spend the years ahead cleaning up after Doctor Hall in the daytime and helping him to sleep at night. 'Teapots always win. They know how to bully anyone they fancy. And I don't have no one to help me. If Irish was here, I could solve the problem of Sticky Fingers with her penny whistle. All I'd have to do is tell him I had it off with three or four convict men who come to the Factory and he'd have to go off looking for someone else so as he could empty his teapot. The butler was the same. That's all teapots think about – their stupid spout.'

There was not long to wait. Doctor Hall came to the doorway and entered. Mrs Douglass heard him coming and quickly turned to Ann. She flicked her head towards the back door and Ann hurried off, but not so far that she couldn't hear any of the conversations.

Doctor Douglass walked into the big room, smiled at Doctor Hall and bade him good morning. 'Doctor Hall, I am surprised you could arrive so early. Welcome to my house.'

Mrs Douglass moved closer to them and nodded a welcome to Doctor Hall.

Doctor Hall smiled at Mrs Douglass. 'Thank you, Mrs Douglass, for your invitation to talk over matters here in Parramatta and Sydney. I am pleased to see that you have a comfortable house and not too far from the Factory.'

Mrs Douglass returned his compliment and said something about their house being somewhat primitive. 'But you soon adjust to new conditions.'

Ann and Mary pressed their ears to the door. They heard everything. Ann was a twinge disappointed when she heard Doctor Douglass acting in a friendly fashion to Hall. She had been hoping for a showdown with shouting and bad language – even threats. She couldn't understand how men who everyone said would be enemies could chat on as if the weather was the only thing worth discussing.

The voice of Mrs Douglass was different. It still had the high pitch of a well-off woman, but there was an edge of flint coming through. Doctor Hall seemed to ignore her.

Ann and Mary stared into each other's faces at the door, occasionally flashing the sign of impending action in the big room.

Then, quite suddenly, Mrs Douglass spoke out strongly to her husband that she had an urgent job for Willy Bragge to feed a new horse. She left immediately by the open front doorway. Both girls exchanged looks of confusion. They soon understood. They heard Doctor Douglass enquire of Doctor Hall if there were any topics of interest on the voyage out. He asked how many female convicts were on the *Mary Anne.*

'We had 108, mostly young women, and we suffered only one death.'

'And the cause of that?'

'Mostly caused by malnutrition over recent years. A fatal combination of bad food, alcohol and sloth.'

'A very bad mixture.'

'I tried to save the poor wretch, but she was beyond the reach of medicine. And once the fever set in, we had no real hope.'

'I understand. And how was the general behaviour?'

'Quite amenable to discipline. We had no floggings. But allow me to bring up the reason for my visit this morning. It concerns the situation of one particular female convict.'

'Please do.'

Behind the door, Mary pointed her finger at Ann and nodded. Ann nodded back, knowing the battle was about to open up.

'Her name is Ann Rumsby. She is a girl of some eighteen to twenty years of age, and I believe she had been treated very badly by the court in Norwich.'

There was a pause while Doctor Douglass twice repeated the name Rumsby as if trying to remember something. 'Doctor Hall,' he started, 'I think I have met this convict girl. My wife gave her shelter here in this house, though I must say I have hardly spoken to the girl. Why your special interest?'

'Doctor Douglass, I am moved by your sense of charity, especially that of Mrs Douglass. I know the girl in question to be highly intelligent, though utterly illiterate. However, she is diligent in her prayers and is capable of reform into an honest and worthwhile citizen. I should also add that despite what is noted about her being a whore, she is still a virgin.'

'Quite an interesting contradiction. Doctor Hall.'

The two girls managed to control their need to giggle.

'Doctor Hall,' he continued, 'virginity in Parramatta is a valued but rare condition. It is also difficult to recognise. It is not stamped on their faces. You have some evidence, or hearsay, concerning this girl?'

'Yes, in the case of Ann Rumsby, I know her virginity to be proven.'

'I admire your academic acumen, Doctor Hall, but allow me to tell you that I even know of two married women who both claimed to be virgin. I also had one male convict, a gardener here, who slept with the same Irish girl three times in the one week and each time she claimed to be a virgin and charged accordingly.'

'That may be so, Doctor Douglass. The Irish cannot be trusted, but in the case of Ann Rumsby, who is in fact, and thankfully, English, I know she is an honest virgin.'

'I take your word for it, but how could you be so sure?'

'Because I tested every woman on the *Mary Anne*.'

'How did you do that?'

'By physical examination.'

'By what procedure?

'By digital examination.'

'With your hand?'

'Yes, with one finger.'

Ann and Mary raised their eyebrows as if disputing the one-finger efforts of Doctor Hall.

'In an effort to clear up any possible problems, I examined every female convict.'

'I must say I laud your perseverance. Then how many virgins did you find in this way?'

'Out of 108, only two confirmed virgins. Many professed virginity, but I could not verify their claims.'

'I'm fascinated. Did you encounter bleeding?'

'No. As soon as I felt tissue, I withdrew my finger.'

'Remarkable sensitivity, Doctor Hall. I am increasingly impressed, although I must point out, as I am sure you already know, that the absence of the hymen does not, in itself, prove that the girl is not a virgin.'

'That is true, but it is the only definite proof of virginity I could provide.'

'And what happened with the second virgin you found on the ship?'

'The girl was foolish. She sold herself to several sailors all over the ship. A frightful hussy. I lost interest in her completely. There are some people who just cannot be helped, I'm afraid.'

'But not so Ann Rumsby?'

'No, not Ann Rumsby. I took it upon myself as her spiritual guide to nurture her honesty and together we practised the arts of writing and reading. The girl can now write out the opening lines of the Lord's Prayer. Her handwriting is still clumsy but, with practice, she will certainly improve in all directions.'

'Did any of the females on the *Mary Anne* complain about your examinations?'

'Some did. In fact, I often had to resort to having two sailors hold such women in position. However, despite the need to use force, no female was injured under my care.'

'So what are you proposing this morning?'

'I am simply requesting that the convict girl Ann Rumsby be transported from this house to my newly acquired residence in Sydney. Her education is nowhere near complete and, as my domestic servant, she will be given regular instruction. She has a great desire to learn reading.'

'I am sure she has. But I must point out that through lengthy conversations she has had with my wife, Ann Rumsby has indicated that she does not wish to be removed from this house.'

'Doctor Douglass, I am amazed that you could take on such an attitude. The girl is a convict and preliminary arrangements have been made to have her assigned to my house as a domestic servant.'

'And no doubt you have spoken to other authorities?'

'Most certainly. I have explained my position to the Reverend Samuel Marsden. He is a man of God and he applauds my efforts to help this convict girl.'

'I'm sure he does. But I am afraid I cannot allow the convict girl to be quartered in your Sydney house. We can of course be careful how we handle this situation.'

'There is only one way to handle this situation. You simply hand the girl over into my care and let's be done with it.'

'I'm afraid I cannot do that. As you may well know, I am a magistrate, along with Samuel Marsden, and I must point out that this convict girl has made a complaint against you, concerning your, shall we say, digital handling of her on the *Mary Anne*. I believe you became besotted with the girl and wished to indulge in coitus. That is perfectly understandable. You are a young man and she is a very attractive, indeed nubile, young woman. However, rather than resurrecting your rather sordid history of the *Mary Anne* and the entire complement of female convicts, you should quietly leave this house and drop any plan of availing yourself of the body or services of Ann Rumsby.'

'Doctor Douglass, I am horrified by your changing attitude. I have no intention with regard to Ann Rumsby other than to promote her formal education and religious instruction.' Doctor Hall stiffened and stepped back as if preparing for a physical assault. 'I can barely believe what I am hearing. Sir, I am shocked to hear myself demanding an apology. You have insulted me to the very core of my being. Me! I am not only a surgeon, but an English gentleman and a practising Christian!'

Doctor Douglass nodded his understanding, but remained calm, probably aware that both Ann Rumsby and Mary Wooten were close by and listening to every word. 'Doctor Hall, I understand your hurt. However, in order to avoid a sordid scandal in this small community, I urge you to forget Ann Rumsby and to throw yourself into your professional work here in this new colony. I am sure you have much to offer, though I would recommend you rethink your desperation in finding virgins.'

Doctor Hall began to shake slightly as if he were either slightly cold, or about to explode into a temper. 'Douglass, I demand you release Ann Rumsby. If you do so, I see no need to take any further action.'

'Doctor Hall, I am sorry to disappoint you, but Ann Rumsby will stay here under the direction of Mrs Douglass.'

The two men carried on their argument, with Doctor Hall increasingly furious and Doctor Douglass calm and definite. He was not going to release Ann Rumsby.

Behind the door, Ann and Mary stared, eyes wide open, into each other's face. Mary's face bubbled with happiness. She felt certain she would be able to work with her friend and she nodded to Ann and gave a cheerful thumbs-up. Unfortunately, her fist struck Ann lightly on the nose. Both of them had to stifle a giggle.

Mrs Douglass arrived back with another man. She swished straight into the room, took in the stormy situation and tried to calm the atmosphere. 'I was wondering if either of you surgeons would like a cup of tea?' she asked.

Doctor Douglass said yes, while Doctor Hall murmured something neither girl could follow.

'Then, Doctor Hall, perhaps you would like something stronger, though I'm afraid my dear husband has only a supply of rum.'

'Thank you, Mrs Douglass, but you should know that I am a man who has sworn off the drinking of alcohol. However, please don't let me stop anyone who feels the need for refreshment.'

Doctor Douglass smiled at the impasse. 'Doctor Hall, you will realise that my wife and I have caught the Irish contagion for endless cups of tea. Though I must say I do have a weakness for rum and raspberry at the end of the day. There is very little here in this colony by way of convivial entertainment.'

Mrs Douglass seemed to calm the situation and immediately started on an anecdote about the early years of the settlement. 'You must have heard, Doctor Hall, of the famous dog races that were popular with the First Fleet.'

Doctor Hall waved as if he wanted to speak, but Mrs Douglass kept on.

'The officers had decided, by way of entertainment, to hold a dog race with a monetary prize. Many convicts were given the job of carrying the drinks and nibbles. Apparently, they did a good job of it because while the officers and the free settlers were enjoying a few too many drinks, another group of convicts relieved themselves of their shackles, nabbed the best dog and proceeded to kill, cook and eat the beast. I'm afraid that rather stopped public celebrations for some time after that.'

Doctor Hall tried to smile; Douglass forced himself to laugh and was joined by the man who had entered with Mrs Douglass. Both Ann and Mary clapped a hand over their mouths to muffle any giggle.

Doctor Hall objected to the presence of a convict in the conversation.

Mary leaned in to Ann. 'He's going on about Willy Bragge. Willy's one of us.'

Ann didn't understand, but nodded that she'd agree with anything.

Mrs Douglass clapped her hands for silence and in her most piercing Irish accent she turned on Dr Hall. 'Doctor Hall, in my house, I am happy to have my convict servant Willy Bragge as my personal assistant. And I would like you to know that if your glorious British Empire, which means English Empire, were to have servants and officials as honest and as valuable as Willy Bragge, the world would be a wonderful and peaceful place. So Willy Bragge will remain.'

'I am sorry, Mrs Douglass, if I disturbed you, but I have been the virtual guardian of Ann Rumsby during months at sea and in recompense for the unjustifiable sentence passed on her in Norfolk I have arranged that I would continue her education in Sydney. She will be cared for and treated with my most sincere respect.'

'That would have been a good start, but it won't happen. I can assure you that Ann Rumsby will remain dutifully employed in this house, with me,' said Mrs Douglass.

Doctor Hall went red in the face again and a thin white line of froth began to appear between his clenched lips. The girls behind the door couldn't see such a fury, but they heard his words and the fire of the man's anger seared through the door. Doctor Hall burst into a froth of anger and started to rattle off his accusation of a collusion of Doctor and Mrs Douglass against him.

The girls were thrilled with the morning's entertainment and they patted each other on the head as a quick celebration.

However, the scene didn't last long. There was a noise at the door and the girls heard another man stomp into the big room.

The new man had a towering voice and he roared his demands. 'Doctor Douglass, what is this disturbance, and in front of this convict servant? And you, Mrs Douglass, I know that you would have tried to quell this disagreement.'

The man would have gone on and on, but was cut short by Mrs Douglass.

'Reverend Marsden, please feel welcome in my home, and I am sorry you have arrived during a discussion between my husband and Doctor Hall. I presume you have already met Doctor Hall.'

'Yes, Mrs Douglass, I have already met Doctor Hall, a man I have found to be of impeccable manners. And thank you, Mrs Douglass, for your welcome. However, I am afraid I have come in the midst of an argument of a heated nature.'

Doctor Douglass immediately thanked Marsden for his visit and tried to outline the current problem. 'Mr Marsden, I am afraid that Doctor Hall and I have come to a disagreement over a certain convict servant.'

'Thank you, Doctor Douglass. I hope that as a fellow magistrate with you, I might be able to help ease the problem. Who is the said servant?'

Doctor Hall cut in with 'A female convict named Ann Rumsby,

Reverend Marsden. I point out that this female convict was under my care on the *Mary Anne*. She had been in poor health and I was able to ease that problem. And in that time I found her to be responsive to spiritual care with a desire to reform her life and acquire education.'

'A worthy association between doctor and patient, Doctor Hall. I presume you wish to continue your help in regard to this convict?'

'Yes, Reverend Marsden, such is my profound wish.'

'Then what hinders that wish, Doctor Hall?'

'I do,' interrupted Mrs Douglass.

Marsden looked at Mrs Douglass and Doctor Douglass with a sign of eager interest. 'Mrs Douglass, am I to understand that this convict servant is Irish?'

'No, Mr Marsden. The girl is English, well, from Norfolk, and I believe that the Norfolk people are probably as much Dutch as they are English.'

'That may well be the case, but the important concern is that she is not Irish.'

'No, Mr Marsden, you may sleep well at night, utterly relaxed. She is certainly not Irish. I have not heard her sing or recite beautiful poetry, or even use logic in her conversations, so she has the characteristics of the Imperial English race.'

Marsden swallowed hard then looked around the room in dismay, as if trying to find some hidden, but unknown object. He seemed uncertain as to what Mrs Douglass actually meant. 'Thank you, Mrs Douglass. But please can we come to the crux of my being here. Let me ask you, Doctor Douglass, as a fellow magistrate, what is the problem with this so-called English convict?'

Doctor Douglass beamed a smile and seemed more than happy. 'It is all very simple, my dear Marsden. Mrs Douglass and I have decided it would be in the interests of the female convict Ann Rumsby that she remain in this household. According to Doctor Hall, the girl is a virgin and so my wife and I are sure that we could arrange a marriage with a worthy man and so help her lead a safe and useful life.'

Marsden moved his face as if trying to chew something. He rocked slightly from side to side before answering. 'Douglass, I thought we had survived the "Love your convicts" with the departure of Macquarie. So I am perplexed. I was of the opinion that this Rumsby convict was assigned to the Female Factory and she is to be reassigned as a domestic servant to Doctor James Hall.'

Doctor Douglass quickly replied. 'That was also our understanding. However, I am afraid that this convict girl has made a complaint against the name of Doctor Hall and my wife and I would prefer that the girl remain in this house until such time as this disagreement is settled and everyone is happy.'

Marsden's face rippled slightly with anger. He shifted his weight from foot to foot and for a few moments he seemed lost for a logical reply.

Doctor Hall had remained silent and tense, spoke as if he had trouble controlling his passion. He seemed to chew over each word before speaking. 'Mister Marsden, I am happy to concur with your every word. Only yesterday, I had words with Ann Rumsby and she informed me that she was nervous in this house due to her belief that Doctor Douglass would bring about her ruin.'

Mrs Douglass gasped with shock and muttered a string of Gaelic swear words. Doctor Douglass blushed at his wife's language and would have spoken but Marsden raised his hand for silence and turned to the male convict standing close by.

'Convict, bring the female convict Ann Rumsby into this room.'

Willy Bragge looked to Mrs Douglass for permission to move. Mrs Douglass nodded and Willy Bragge walked to the inside door. He felt the scurry on the other side of the door and paused to push it open. Ann and Mary were flattened against the side wall looking fearfully at Bragge. He took Ann by the upper arm and led her into the big room.

The atmosphere in the room was as tense as violin strings. Marsden looked at the girl with near hatred. Mrs Douglass remained calm and Doctor Hall tried to manage a weak smile. He moved to Ann and took her by the other arm as if to lead her out of the house. But Willy Bragge did not let go. In fact, he tugged her closer to himself. Doctor Hall tried to tug her harder, without success. Willy Bragge jerked Ann to himself and half turned on Doctor Hall.

Hall was overcome with fury. 'Convict,' he roared, 'I will not be threatened. I will have you flogged.'

Doctor Douglass stepped in and demanded both men release Ann. 'While this convict is in this house, I will have no talk of flogging.'

Hall immediately struggled to regain an even temper. 'I apologise for my tone. However, I am not accustomed to being in competition with a convict who I suspect has his own unhealthy interest in Ann Rumsby.

Mrs Douglass shook her head. 'Doctor Hall, please allow me to tell you that our convict servant Bragge has many interests, but at present, Ann Rumsby is not on the list. However, I would be happy if we could continue this conversation some other time. This girl has been in this miserable colony no more than a week or so and I will be happy to teach her whatever I can.'

She might have gone on, but Marsden waved his hands as if such an action would put a stop to all conversation. He almost succeeded, but Hall was determined to recover his control over Ann.

'Reverend Marsden,' he started, 'please put a stop to this obfuscation and support my claim to have Ann Rumsby assigned to my house. Allow me to talk directly to the convict woman in the presence of all of us.'

'Please do,' interjected Mrs Douglass.

Hall turned to Ann, but was cut off by Marsden.

'Doctor Hall, I believe I am the correct person to interview this convict. You are, shall we say, too full of the milk of human kindness. Put your faith in God and your high motives will be rewarded.'

Hall gestured that he would surrender his option in favour of Marsden.

Reverend Marsden took a step towards Ann Rumsby. Ann tried to stake a step back, but was barked at by Marsden to stand still. She did so with a look of fear shrouding her face.

Marsden half smiled at her. 'There is no need for fear. Not yet anyway.' He reached over with the index finger of his podgy hand and touched her skin, just below her neck. 'You have the skin of youth,' he started. He then moved his hand across the skin above her breasts watching the skin stretch under his finger. 'Doctor Douglass,' he started, 'this heifer has come from a good paddock. You have been feeding her well. Hard work will rid her of her puppy softness. But above all that, she has the crafty look of the Irish about her. Most probably some of her antecedents migrated from that bog, to take up an easier life in Norfolk. She is from Norfolk, you say. But I will tell you that were you to scratch back a few generations you would unearth the brutality of that degenerate race. So for me this woman is Irish.'

Ann straightened up as if in a bad temper. 'You can make up anything you like about anyone you don't like, but you are stupid. I am from Norfolk.'

'What did you call me?'

'I didn't call you anything, but the women in the factory say to keep out of your way, because you is a stupid flogging parson.'

'How dare you insult me,' he screamed in her face. 'You will begin to learn English manners right here in Parramatta. What do you make of me now?'

'I am sure you would make a good butler. Butlers are good at making up things.'

Marsden raised his hand to slap her face, but stopped. 'Bragge,' he shouted, 'Bragge, knock this convict down!'

Doctor Hall started to intervene, but was stopped by Marsden. No one else moved.

Marsden shouted at Bragge, 'Convict, do your duty. Exorcise the wickedness from this Irish woman. Strike her!' His last words were more of a shriek than words.

Willy Bragge took a step towards Ann, who stiffened as if fearless. Her eyes concentrated on Willy Bragge, willing him to do his worst.

Mrs Douglass tried to have the vicious charade stopped, but was again stopped by Marsden. The reverend raised his hand and again screamed at Willy to strike.

Willy moved like an athlete, drew back his right arm and swung it with force against Ann Rumsby. The smack caught her by the neck and her jaw. She went down without a sound and lay crumpled and silent on the floor. Mrs Douglass swore in Gaelic and crossed herself. Marsden watched her action with horror. He might have said something, but was distracted by something about Ann.

Ann lay still for moments then began to quietly whimper in shock.

Marsden again addressed Willy, 'Convict, you may as well finish the job.' He pointed to Ann's legs, uncovered by her fall. 'You will see, convict, that this female is wearing more garments than are unacceptable under local rules. See she is wearing an under dress. It will be held by a tie at the waist. They cannot stop flaunting themselves. Bragge, bend down and rip that garment from her.'

Willy looked around for support. 'I would rather not,' he said quietly. 'She has done me no harm.'

Marsden shouted at him to do his convict duty. Willy shrugged, bent down and gathered a fistful of underdress and tugged. It came free and he left it on the floor. Mrs Douglass immediately stepped over and retrieved the thin garment and rolled it in her hands. Ann began to whimper more loudly, which seemed to annoy Marsden.

'She sounds Irish. That blubbering sound is a form of Irish language. Bragge, wake her out of it.'

Willy didn't move.

'Bragge, you are a good footman. Did you see how easily that undergarment slid from her body. There was nothing to stop it. Like most of the Irish women, this convict does not wear pantaloons, or any such thing. These women are a blot on the decency of this colony. So, convict Bragge, you have narrowly escaped a flogging already, escape another one now. Wake her from her pretence of injury. Use your footwork.'

'I beg your pardon, Mr Marsden, what do you order me to do?'

'Use your foot, man. Lay your foot into that Irish backside with some force. Do it now.'

No one moved. Hall tried to step forward but was stopped by a simple wave of Marsden's hand.

'Now!' screamed Marsden.

Willy took a step forward and swung his foot into a kick against Ann's bottom. The kick, a well-placed move, mostly crashed on the floor, but part of it bounced Ann a few inches across the room.

'And again,' screamed Marsden, but Ann was well and truly awake.

She moved into a sitting position and Mrs Douglass stepped in to help her stand.

Marsden shouted, 'Don't allow yourself to display a weakness, Mrs Douglass. This convict will deceive you.'

Mrs Douglass was holding Ann by the upper arm and silently swore in Gaelic. 'I think I can be the arbiter of that,' she said quietly, then added, 'I believe God is Irish.'

Marsden began to splutter about blasphemy, but Doctor Hall seemed to come out of some stupor and broke into the action. 'I will take this convict into my service,' he said weakly and tried to pull Ann away from Mrs Douglass.

Mrs Douglass was not prepared to give ground. 'The best thing you can do, Doctor Hall, is to take the Reverend Marsden and quietly leave this house. Both of you, leave in peace and as soon as possible.'

Marsden stood shaking with anger. He roared, 'I demand that this convict is given into my charge and under the direction of our greatly respected friend, Doctor James Hall.'

Mrs Douglass stiffened. 'That may well be the case. But it will not happen today. Nor will it happen tomorrow, neither tomorrow nor any other day in the near future.'

Ann regained her senses and quietly spoke out. 'No one has ever struck me like that. Not even my own father. You will be sorry for what you have done, Mr Marsden.'

Marsden answered in cold fury, 'I apologise only to God. And had your feeble-headed father taken an interest in your discipline, he might have saved you from a life of crime. To you, Doctor Hall, we shall take our leave, to organise the release of this convict woman from this house.

Doctor Douglass, you shame us all. You a revered magistrate in this colony and you should study your conscience and pray for guidance on this matter.' Without more words, but a lot of shaking, the parson spun on his heel and left the house.

Doctor Hall gave a slight bow to Mrs Douglass, turned and followed Marsden like a faithful dog.

Ann stood with Mrs Douglass and looked with barely controlled horror at Willy Bragge. It took some time for her to bring herself to speak. 'You great smelly thug, you coulda killed me.'

'I'm sure he was careful, Ann,' said Mrs Douglass.

Doctor Douglass gave a short cough, opened his mouth to say something but changed his mind and turned to walk out of the room leaving the inside door open. Mary nervously walked in, afraid to look at Ann.

'I tried me best,' said Willy. 'But she don't help.' He stood like a guilty-looking schoolboy. 'Honest, Mrs Douglass, I tried to make it look good and all she had to do was ride out the smack, but she don't do nothing of the sort. Instead she goes all stiff and cops it full on the neck.'

Ann wasn't interested in excuses. 'It wasn't just me neck. I thought you broke me jaw. And now I even got a loose tooth. I can wiggle it with me tongue.'

Mrs Douglass stepped in closer to try and calm Ann. 'Show me which tooth and let's hope we can save it.'

Ann stood with her mouth open. Mrs Douglass took hold of Ann's jaw to open the mouth further. 'There's a lot of good teeth in there, Ann Rumsby. They tell me that girls with frizzy hair usually have good teeth. You're lucky. Now, which tooth is it?'

'It's the one on the side at the back. Put your finger in and you'll feel it. It's the only one what's loose.'

'Well then, then let's see. Just as well I was washing my hands just before all this commotion.'

Mrs Douglass stretched an elegant forefinger into Ann's open mouth, moving across the molars until she found the tooth with just the slightest movement. 'That's the one, well enough. It's hardly moving and I think it will settle down. Just chew on the other side of your face. I think you're lucky. And you're not even Irish. And Willy Bragge, next time you're forced into something like this, concentrate on where you land the blow. And you make a sound as though all your energies were involved in the strike. Is that possible? And you, Ann Rumsby, learn how to take a blow – to ride it out like a prize fighter. Not enough girls learn how to fight and counterpunch. It's a pity.'

Willy looked increasingly sheepish as though ashamed of his actions. He looked at Mrs Douglass as if asking if he might speak. Mrs Douglass nodded.

Willy coughed and started as if making a big speech. 'Let me tell you what, Miss Frizzy Hair of the loose tooth. If that tooth gives you more trouble like, and moves about a lot, I know an Irish pal in Sydney who can fix it for you.'

'I'm certain you do, Willy Bragg,' said Mrs Douglass, 'but in the meantime let's get Ann Rumsby moving about.' She took hold of Ann under the right armpit and started to walk her around the room.

By the second turn of the room, Ann was feeling safe on her feet and the dizzy sensations were gone. She spoke back to Willy over her shoulder. 'I wonder what magic trick your Irish pal can bring off. What's he do?'

'Well, he's a big man, even if he is Irish. What he does first is to stretch you out, face up, on the floor, or outside under some sort of shady tree, then he more or less sits on your chest with his knees on your shoulders to stop you getting in the way. Then he opens your mouth with his fingers, finds the bad tooth and he just pulls it out with his special pair of lifters.'

'What's his special lifters?'

'If you just listen, Fuzzy, I'll tell you. His special lifters are like pliers, but the working end is bent and the clamps are sort of rounded. Anyway, they fit over the tooth. He gets a good grip and rocks the tooth a bit to see how strong it is. If the tooth is strong enough, he puts on the pressure and twists and lifts at the same time. If he has a helper, the second person holds the head down on the floor. You can hear the tooth breaking loose from the jaw and the next thing the trouble is over, he shows the tooth to the man, or woman, and he gets off. Then he puts out his hand for a couple of dumps. The man who's just lost his tooth, he does a lot of spitting and he's off to work again. How's that?'

'Sounds wonderful, Willy,' said Mrs Douglass, though her face told the world that she was horrified, and she started mumbling about 'life among savages'.

Ann simply said she was sure that her tooth would recover. 'But apart from that,' she went on, 'if ever I have to make use of your Irish pal, I'll make sure he takes out one of yours first, Willy Bragge.'

'Dear God, Ann Rumsby, you do make your life difficult!' Mrs Douglass might have gone on, but was interrupted by the return of Doctor Douglass.

Doctor Douglass moved to stand beside the big table. He looked from each of the trio on the room, but finally concentrating his attention on Ann. 'Ann Rumsby, I am sorry to note that you have met our resident flogging parson, the Reverend Samuel Marsden. Unfortunately, he is also our most outstanding magistrate, a man who holds the lives of many convicts and free settlers at his whim. He has met today with our struggle for your future life with Doctor James Hall. Marsden will seek this opportunity to maintain his power over the law and his struggle with the governor himself. We must be very careful.'

Mrs Douglass put her arm around the shoulders of Ann and looked to her husband. 'What about Doctor Hall? What do you say about him?'

'I say nothing much, except that Doctor Hall will see himself as a victim. He will become the ammunition that Marsden needs. Marsden will fight the progressives using the body of Doctor Hall. All I can say at this juncture is that Ann Rumsby must maintain a low profile. Willy, wherever Ann goes, make quite sure she is always well within eyesight.'

Willy nodded, and would have gone on, but for Ann who spoke out. 'And Willy Bragge, You can be within eyesight, but keep yourself at arm's length.'

Willy smiled and nodded.

Doctor Douglass asked after Andrew White and was told he had gone into Parramatta with a letter from Mrs Douglass.

'Then we must all get busy. I am expecting a special visit from the Governor, Sir Thomas Brisbane. He wants to discuss my idea of a university here in Sydney.'

'Right,' ordered Mrs Douglass, 'I'm sure his excellency will be enraptured by such an idea. You could both discuss it for the next hundred years. In the meantime, Ann, find Mary and make this room bright and shiny. And when the governor is here, just do two things; look smart, and then look busy!'

11

The Governing Teapot

There was a thunder of horses accompanied by an all-in chorus of barking dogs from up and down the river. The sound changed to an instant squealing of brakes and the commands of a driver to 'Come by and whoa'. The combined sound was greater than the sight of it all and Ann realised she was about to be swirled up, close and personal to Australian royalty.

The governor, Sir Thomas Brisbane, had arrived with due pomp and ceremony to the not so glorious front gate. His open carriage was hauled by four sweaty horses adorned with all the plumes and fancy harness of a royal carriage. The driver sat on the high seat up front beside a man with a polished musket. Two footmen in scarlet jackets sat on the high seat at the back looking as if they were pretending to be statues.

Governor Brisbane sat alone, deep inside the carriage. He barely looked around, but waited for a footman to jump down from the back seat, run around to open the carriage door, lower the step and then stand rigidly to attention. The governor alighted from the phaeton, stood in the roadway and slowly looked around. Only then did he take his feather bonnet from under his left arm and placed it carefully on his head. The feathers barely moved in the breeze. However, despite the cool autumnal morning, all five men were sweating in their smart uniforms.

Doctor Douglass rushed through the front yard and shouted over his shoulder for Mrs Douglass to drop everything and to join him at the gate. Mathew ordered the girls to hurry out, to look tidy and had them stand in line, beside the ever yawning open front door.

Doctor Douglass saluted the governor. Mrs Douglass beamed smiles and welcomes as she ushered their visitor through the nondescript garden, through the open doorway and, once inside, flustered about ordering the girls back to the kitchen. Willy went off with the driver and two footmen in the direction of the stables. There, the horses would be watered, the carriage dusted and the men given mugs of ale.

Ann smiled as she headed for the kitchen. The sight of the overdressed men and the polished carriage almost reminded her of Norfolk, but the image didn't match. Nothing except the footman stood straight, let alone to any sort of attention. Nor did the surroundings help. For her, the untidy-looking trees set their stamp on confusion. None of them stood in rows as if they had just grown without any order. And they were messy. Some had their bark hanging in steamers from spindly branches and, most of all, their very trunks stood about in twisted shapes and sizes. There were just too many messy pictures. Even the raggedy split-rail fences seemed to serve no real purpose, while the nondescript neighbouring houses stood apart from each other with front doors that were never shut. For Ann, it was all unreal. It was as though the official party was really nothing more than a mob of overdressed characters from some travelling pantomime.

But the governor was real enough. He marched into the house, through the open door, as if he had been there many times before. Mary had already placed two more chairs in the position where Mrs Douglass had sat sewing the day when Ann first entered the house. The governor sat on the centre chair and as he sat his medals clanked on his jacket and his sword scraped the floor beside his legs.

Doctor Douglass started a speech of welcome which was cut short by Sir Thomas. 'My dear Douglass, thank you for your wonderful hospitality and your outstanding achievements in this little colony. Please sit here with me. However, I must tell you that on my way this morning, somewhere about that tedious halfway place they call Auburn, I happened to pass a carriage with none other than our esteemed magistrate, the Reverend Samuel Marsden. As usual, he smiled, but today he gave me the impression of a man who had eaten too much and in consequence had a bellyful of gas, but could find no quiet place to arrange relief.'

Mrs Douglass blushed while her husband chuckled. But he was quick to outline the recent visit of Marsden.

'Only this morning, the reverend flogger was here with a Doctor James Hall. Hall arrived on the *Mary Anne* as surgeon.

'Douglass, I have heard of this man Hall. He is apparently very good with his hands, is he not?'

'Sir Thomas, I believe that such is the case.'

'Is there more than mere hearsay on this matter?'

'Well, your excellency, I have confirmation on the word of the doctor himself and further confirmed by at least two of his female convicts from the *Mary Anne*.'

'Exactly what was confirmed, Doctor Douglass?'

'That he followed a procedure of establishing whether a female convict was a virgin or not. Apparently he carried out his digital examinations on every female convict on the *Mary Anne*.'

'Sounds like a full-time job. And why so thorough? But was he successful?'

'Probably.'

'Probably? I think we need something more specific than probably.'

'Your excellency, the absence of a hymen is no proof that a girl is not a virgin. I am sure that many girls lose their hymen long before marriage or any sexual contact.'

'But it's pretty weighty evidence that if, in fact, the girl is known to have an intact hymen, she definitely is a virgin. Is that correct?'

'Quite.'

'Douglass, I cannot believe that this Hall fellow methodically carried out these investigations just for the pleasure of dominating women. I cannot believe him to be just a collector, someone with a record number of discovered virgins to his collection. Is there more to this story?'

'I am sure there is and I am sure I know the answer.'

'Then please tell me.'

'I am sure that our Doctor Hall is mortally afraid of an infection which can be transmitted via physical contact with a human being who is not a virgin.'

The governor lowered his voice and almost whispered to Doctor Douglass, 'Douglass, are you talking about the disease called syphilis?'

'Precisely.'

'Well, he has every reason to be afraid. The disease has already killed off almost one-quarter of men and women throughout Europe. It's almost as bad as the plague.'

'And as yet, we have no cure.'

'Well then, I should be more than interested to meet one of these virgins. It should be noted that this must be something of a rarity in Parramatta, is it not? But please forgive me, Mrs Douglass. This conversation must be most unpleasant to your ears.'

'It is certainly unpleasant, but necessary to establish that any young woman should not be abandoned to a lowlife.'

'Is this Doctor Hall a lowlife?'

'He is listed as a gentleman, but he has the characteristics of that other description. No doubt he is capable of reform.'

'Mrs Douglass, I admire your spirit of generosity. But please, I want details as to what may have passed in this house.'

Doctor Douglass quickly explained how Hall and Marsden arrived with the intention of transporting the convict girl, Ann Rumsby, to Sydney under the pretence of Ann becoming his domestic servant. The governor sat and listened. He even winced at the description of Willy Bragge being ordered by Marsden to knock the girl to the floor and then giving her a good kicking.

The governor nodded as if understanding. 'And how is this convict girl now?'

Mrs Douglas replied very carefully, 'She is shaky, though I am sure she will recover. You will see her yourself in a few moments. Unfortunately, Marsden seems to believe her to be Irish and therefore in need of special treatment. Given the slightest excuse, he will have the girl flogged.'

The governor looked at his boots and shook his head. 'These men of God. They don't seem to know the word compassion. Is the girl Catholic?'

Mrs Douglass shook her head. 'Thank God she is not Catholic. If she were, in this land of Marsden's, her life would be Hell on Earth. She is from Norfolk and has been more or less attached to the English Church.'

'Mrs Douglass, you are Irish, but not Catholic.'

'Culturally I am Catholic and politically I sympathise with Irish Catholics, but I am Church of Ireland. Many in my family are Catholics, though my father who was Church of Ireland was an apothecary, and a very good one.'

'You are also an apothecary?'

'For my sins, yes. But I lack the experience of my father. I have had to learn from my esteemed husband, who says he is English, except that he has a Scottish name and he was born in Ireland.'

'This might explain some of the frictions between your husband and our dear Samuel Marsden. I'm afraid that Marsden sees anything he dislikes as Irish. Most screaming preachers see the Devil behind anything they don't like. But Marsden only sees the Irish. It's a pity that the population of this colony is almost half Irish free settlers and Irish convicts. I'm afraid the growing population gives Marsden great scope for hatred.'

The three sat discussing the Irish question for most of the morning. It was when Mrs Douglass offered refreshments that Ann was to meet the governor.

Mrs Douglass went to the kitchen only to find Ann and Mary busy scrubbing the bench. Mrs Douglass smiled, certain that the pair had just started such a job, and had spent much of their time listening at the door. 'Ann,' she ordered, 'bring the drinks on a tray. And Mary, make tea for three. Bring the drinks first and use the best glasses.'

Mrs Douglass returned to the front room, to hear her husband and the governor discussing the possibility of setting up a university. The governor was enthusiastic and suggested that perhaps another magistrate, William Wentworth, might also be interested in such a cultural adventure.

Doctor Douglass tried to look enthusiastic, but failed.

'You doubt the value of involving Wentworth in such an adventure? I would have thought you would be interested in anyone of value.'

'I certainly am and I would be delighted if Wentworth were to be involved. However, I feel certain that being a fellow magistrate, Marsden, would ingratiate himself into any discussion and cause nothing but dissension.'

The conversation would have dragged on, but was interrupted by Ann Rumsby carrying drinks.

'How lovely to be served by such a fair young woman. May I ask if you are Irish?'

'No, sir. I am not Irish but I would not be ashamed of it, even if I were.'

The governor's reply was cut short by Mrs Douglass, who demanded of Ann that she only answer the question and, 'Please refer to our honoured guest as your excellency.'

'I'm sorry, excellent. Will you take a drink?'

'Certainly I will. And what is in it?'

'Mrs Douglass calls it rum and raspberry.'

The governor took a glass, sipped it and smiled his approval. 'And tell me, Miss Rumsby, what do you hope for in this far-flung colony? Are you looking for a husband?'

Ann didn't answer but moved sideways to allow Doctor Douglass and Mrs Douglass to take a drink each from the tray.

The governor was not to be left unanswered. 'Tell me, Miss Rumsby, you are both a nubile and comely young woman. I am sure we could find you a suitable husband.'

'Thank you, your excellenty, but I don't need no teapot.'

'Teapot? What do you mean by teapot?

Doctor Douglass chuckled and explained to the governor that the word teapot only referred to men. 'I believe I am quietly referred to as Doctor Teapot.'

'Douglass, this is marvellous.' And tell me, Miss Rumsby, what variety of teapot am I?'

Mrs Douglass tried to change the subject, but the governor was happy to continue.

'I should love to know.'

'I am sure you are a excellent teapot.'

'Well, that is good to know. So tell me, girl, what else do you do?'

'I am a good sewer.'

'What do you sew?'

'I can make jackets as good as anyone. In Norwich, I had a young soldier boy and I made him a new jacket. He looked smart, he did. I could make you a soldier's jacket, better than the one you got on now.'

Both the doctor and Mrs Douglass jumped to their feet shocked by such impudence. But Ann didn't move. Instead she spoke to the governor and asked if he would mind if she touched his jacket.

The governor immediately stood up, with a slight smile on his face as if he were enjoying some game. 'At your service, madam,' he said.

Ann reached forward and gripped the governor's jacket just above the sword hilt. 'See, that bit is too straight. Each side needs to be taken-in at the waist. Otherwise you look like a tube. If you can get enough stuff, I can make you a new jacket. It will be good enough for you to meet the king. Howe's that?'

The governor sat down amused.

Mrs Douglass sent Ann to the kitchen. She apologised to the governor. 'I'm sorry, your excellency. We have had this girl only a few days and I thought of her as a shy person. I can see she is not so.'

'No, Mrs Douglass, being shy is certainly not one of her obvious attributes. Though I will say that she is indeed comely. That Doctor Hall fellow he must have found her quite a challenge. So, Douglass, you will have to watch that girl or we'll all end up working for her.'

Ann and Mary could hear the conversation through the kitchen door and both almost blurted with laughter at the governor depicting Ann as his future boss. To control their laughter, both scurried through the back door and into the garden, where they could let their laughter loose.

'What will we do if I become the boss of Doctor Hall?'

Mary stopped laughing and allowed instant anger to flare across her face. 'I'd let that man have a choice. Either I cut off his fingers, or I cut off his soup vegetables where he's got them down there.'

'Why wait till I'm his boss?' and both girls laughed with a pretence of shock.

42

The Plot Thickens

For Ann, June was all wrong. Instead of long dreamy summer days with walks in the park and lots of soft sunshine, everything in Parramatta was topsy-turvy. Even the air had a bite in it. Many of the days were sunny, but the nights were so cold they were like a Norfolk winter. In the mornings, the ground was covered with frosts that looked like snow. But there was no snow, just cold. Andrew White tried to explain that the weather in New South Wales was the reverse of what she knew in England. But he couldn't explain why. All he could assure her was that the weather would turn warm again after the windy month of August, while September would be like the beginning of summer in England.

For Ann, none of it made sense, except that she had grown to like the look of some of the bigger trees along the river, and having all the space around the house. And one thing she did love above all else was the cold night sky with all the stars crowded together. They seemed to hang low enough in the sky to settle in the tops of the big trees, and they looked like big lumps of ice. On the nights when the moon was full, she was struck with the beauty and mystery of it. For her, the Parramatta sky was something to compensate for her being so far away from everything she knew. In England, the moon and stars were so far away they might just as well be not there at all.

Over the months, Andrew White and Mary Wooten grew closer together, leaving Ann to herself. Doctor Hall became a serial pest. In theory, he turned up to ask Doctor Douglass about various medicines which were available in the government store. Everyone knew his visits were nothing more than an attempt to contact Ann. Hall was seldom happy and relied on Samuel Marsden for spiritual assistance in everything he attempted. He was able to explain to Marsden that on one occasion he had seen the actual face of God, and therefore felt justified in all his actions. He believed in miracles. Marsden nodded in understanding and promised he would retrieve Ann Rumsby from the evil clutches of the Devil incarnate, Doctor Douglass.

Ann had no thoughts on Doctor Hall, other than the fear of him turning up when no one was around and he would try to talk her into a life of security and love with him. Her image of him was that of a teapot with long fingers and even longer fingernails. At the thought of his fingernails, she wondered if she could defend herself with the use of something like a rolling pin.

On that Thursday morning, she had no special thoughts other than cleaning up the front room and carrying in stove wood from outside. But that morning she had no special job. Willy Bragge had already carried in a huge armload of firewood for the stove and straightaway rushed off to get tidy.

Ann didn't have to stand about for long. Doctor Douglass hurried into the room and sat for his breakfast of bread, a slice of cold mutton and tea. Mrs Douglass hadn't made an appearance and Ann wondered why all the tension. She carried the bread to the table with the bread knife and poured tea for the doctor.

He smiled at her and drank his tea quickly. 'Ann Rumsby,' he said politely, 'as soon as we finish here, get yourself smartened up. Try to do something with your frizzy hair.'

'Yes, Doctor Douglass. Are we expecting the governor, or someone special?'

'No, we are not expecting anyone. But you and I, along with Willy Bragge, are to pay a visit to our infamous magistrate, the Reverend Samuel Marsden. He is expecting me and I want you, at some stage of the proceedings, to join the party.' At the word party, he chuckled. 'Willy will drive us in the gig and you will have a chance to see something of the rest of Parramatta. And if you wish, you can talk to Willy. I am sure he'd like to listen.'

'I don't care if he so wishes or not. I don't want to talk to him. The last time we talked, Marsden had him hit me so hard, I almost lost a good tooth.'

'I hope that such an event won't happen again. But in many respects you have been lucky. Many convict girls have suffered far worse. I'm afraid our dearly beloved Reverend Marsden is over-partial to flogging, especiall if his victim happens to be Irish, or even worse, an English Catholic.'

'I haven't seen many of them lot. But I likes the Irish girl ones. They believe in magic and they is good with their hands.'

'Any other accomplishments?'

'They love music, that's their big thing. On the *Mary Anne* I had a friend who played the tin whistle. She made magic with that thing. When she played, I used to drift off and dream of better places. It was better than sleep-dreaming because I was awake and could stop and start with the music and it would stay with me all day.'

'How did she fare with Doctor Hall?'

'She upset him. She knew more about God than he did and he swore that in New South Wales, he'd have her burned as a witch. And she was a better doctor than him. She saved a couple of girls from him. Just when he thought he had a virgin girl, she'd arrange things.'

'Was he so disappointed?'

'I'll say he was. When Sally got arranged like, he got into such a temper, he even banged his head on the side of the ship. That was the best bit.'

'I would love to know more. Perhaps you could explain all this to Mrs Douglass, who might be able to pass it all to me. I am going to need as much evidence as I can gather. So let's go.' He smiled at Ann, hurried off to say goodbye to Mrs Douglass and returned carrying a bonnet for Ann.

The pair left by the front door. Ann was amazed that the door was actually shut. 'Must be the cold,' she thought, and struggled to get into her bonnet, smiling to herself that it was her borrowing of a bonnet that eventually landed her on the misery of the *Mary Anne* and a complicated life in Parramatta.

They stood at the gate for a few moments complaining of the cold and watching for any sign of life.

Ann heard a horse trotting from behind the stable yards and Willy arrived driving a single horse in the two-wheeler gig. The horse stopped with a shake of the reins and Ann climbed in. There was only one seat, though there was plenty of room for the three of them. Doctor Douglass stepped in last and sat on the left of Ann. She felt she was pressed between two teapots. Willy spoke to the horse, gently flapped the reins up and down and the horse walked off. As they settled on the road, Willy ordered the horse to 'get a move on' and she moved into a trot.

'That's better, Willy,' said Doctor Douglass.

Ann had never before sat in a gig and she liked the sensation of rocking about and the sight of the horse's rump rolling from side to side as they went on.

Willy spoke to her. 'Watch her back legs when we make a hard turn at the next corner.'

Ann looked down, over the top of the splashboard, at the mare's hind legs. In a few yards along the road, Willy shook the reins and ordered the mare to 'Gee-o.' Ann was amazed to see the mare's left hind leg criss-cross in front of the right one, which quickly stretched out in a bigger stride.

'She had to change leg,' he said. 'When we started, she was leading with her left leg, but when we turned to the right, she had to change and lead with her right leg. She's a good goer, this one, does it all without any orders from me.'

Doctor Douglass chuckled at their conversation. 'Ann, you should take lessons from Willy. He's good with horses – try to persuade him to teach you how to ride. It'll come in handy here in Parramatta. Make you independent. It's a frightful inconvenience if a woman can't harness

up a horse or even ride. I know of couples where the wife can't do anything with horses. So she depends utterly on her husband. I think they
end up not getting on at all. Would you like to learn?'

'Doctor Douglass, yes. I would love to know all them things.'

'Then you've a good teacher in Willy Bragge.'

'Be he the only one?'

'Yes, he is. Why such a question?'

Ann turned her face hoping that Willy wouldn't hear her reply. 'The
trouble is he is awful smelly. He scratches all the time with the itch.
And there is something wrong with his face. What's he got?'

'Scrofula, that's all. It will take time to heal. Already the sun here in
New South Wales is solving most of his skin troubles. People come here
with a facial lupus and within a few months of sunshine, it virtually
disappears.'

'Whatever it is, when it's gone, will the smell of him go with it?'

'I'm sure it will. Either that, or you'll get used to it.'

Ann sat, suddenly relaxed, watching the mare's hind legs and, for
the first time, she wondered if the horses working in the streets were
happy to be in Parramatta. Would they rather be living it up on the
south of France or even back in Norfolk? It seemed to her that no creature consented to be sent all the way to New South Wales. 'They is
worse off than convicts.'

'Who is?' asked Willy.

'No one. I was talking to meself.'

'Good idea,' said Willy. 'That way, you always get a good answer.'

Doctor Douglass laughed at the conversation and asked Willy to
stand the mare out the front of the Marsden house. 'You can tie up
there and come inside with me.'

Ann was suddenly afraid. 'What about me? That man will want to
take me over.'

'He may well want such a thing. But you will stay out here and
mind the horse. She won't give you any trouble, but don't get down,
unless you have to go into the bushes. Otherwise just sit here and ad-

mire the countryside. I might have to take you inside during our discussion. And if that happens, I will send Willy out to get you. He will help you down, take you to the door and then wait out here with the mare. You just walk straight in and stand just behind me.' He looked at her and Willy in turn.

Both nodded that they understood and Ann sat, more or less relaxed, in the gig and saw both of then enter through the half-closed door.

Inside, the room was spartan, but Marsden sat at his desk like the emperor of some mighty conglomeration. At the same time, he was eating thinly sliced pieces of pork. For a few moments, his fingers hesitated over the plate of meat, but he coughed a little and continued with a new slice. 'Excuse me, Douglass. At this time of the day, I find it necessary to eat something.'

'Please continue. I hope we have not arrived too early.'

'Thank you, I will continue. Fortunately or unfortunately, my slaughterman arrived yesterday and dressed out two pigs for me. We strung up the carcasses from the tree out the back and I must say that after hanging all night, the meat is very good, Very good indeed. Douglass, you should run a few animals.'

'Thank you, your reverence, but I am not a farmer. For all that, I am happy to see that you are making a great success of farming. You must, by now, be one of the colonies biggest landholders.'

'They say I am. Doctor Douglass, please feel welcome and please be seated. Your man can sit on that stool at the door. I must say I admire your choice in a convict. He's quite an accomplished convict that one. I wish we had more like him. We need more convict labour for our holdings. You cannot run farming without good labour.'

'I would prefer we were getting increasing numbers of free settlers.'

'Perhaps in time, Douglass. In the meantime, we desperately need more free labour. With more free labour, we can expand this colony to become the pride of the Empire. Besides, we are a penal colony.

'I'm afraid that many will not agree with such a definition.'

'In what way?'

'Well, it is costing Westminster a fortune to maintain convicts in this colony. In fact, it is three times more expensive to maintain a convict here than it is to maintain the same person in England. New South Wales is a special colony for a special reason.'

Marsden looked on such a revelation with near horror. 'My dear Douglass, the convicts are here because the prisons and even the barges are full of criminals, many of them Irish. This colony is a dumping ground for ne'er-do-wells and unreformed Catholics who have nothing in their heads but thoughts of murder and pillage. They are dumped here to protect Protestant England and English values.'

'Marsden, they are here in what we used to call Botany Bay for a very special reason.'

'Which is?'

'As a labour force to support the English navy. Convicts in England are fully employed mostly in the production of rope for English ships. England is forever running out of rope. Every big ship has some twenty miles of various ropes just to keep them sailing.'

'I don't believe any of that, Douglass, and even if it were true, then why send convicts all the way to Botany Bay?'

'Because of your fear of Catholics. Not only your fears, from Ireland, but the fear of threats to the entire British Empire. We are here on one shore of the huge Pacific Ocean.'

'Then why such concern?'

'Because England does not rule the Pacific. Look at the map. The entire north Pacific is ruled by Spain and the Spanish king is claiming this country in the name of Spain. After all, it was an admiral of the Spanish navy who gave this land mass a name – Australia.'

Marsden sat staring at his plate of sliced pork, chewing and considering how to defeat the Spanish Catholics, if ever they arrived off his coast. 'I doubt your grasp of history, Douglass. The word Australia is written about in a journal by Sir Joseph Banks when he sailed with Lieutenant Cook to discover and map this coastline. Would you dare to deny the words of Cook and Banks?'

'Certainly not. However, you will admit that British ships have great difficulty in sailing the Pacific. The Spaniards pour across from their new capital in Peru, they find ample food in all the islands to the north. They trade in spice and silks, they have no trouble repairing ships and they outnumber any attempts by British ships to encroach on their pond. So the British government needs a safe port with plentiful supplies of fresh water, abundant food resources, ship repair docks and a support colony populated by hard-working tradesmen and labourers. Do you think your shoplifting and footloose convicts can supply all that?'

'Come what may, Douglass. What I know for certain is that God is on the side of the Protestant forces.'

'Good to know that, Marsden. I will pass on your assurance to my wife. In the meantime, there is no future in trying to fill this colony with convicts. The only hope of a prosperous Australia is to encourage free settlers with the promise of free farmland along the rivers and promise them year-round work, building houses, shops and ships. That's our future.'

'I'm afraid you have an Irish view of the Empire.'

'Mr Marsden, that may well be true. However, I am sure you didn't invite me here to discuss the future of the British Empire.'

'Douglass, you are correct, perfectly correct. There is this other matter that weighs heavily on my mind.'

'And that is?'

'It concerns that convict woman who is domiciled in your house. I believe she is Irish.'

'I presume that you mean the convict girl named Ann Rumsby and she is certainly not Irish. She is from Norwich, the capital of Norfolk, sometimes referred to as East Anglia.'

'That may be so but I am sure that in her antecedents you will find Irish blood. Not only that, but she has been under the care of none other than Doctor James Hall, a man who, through his passion for education, found in her the seed of reformation, a man who has seen the face of God. '

'A rare man.'

Marsden squirmed in his seat, his face reddened with anger and he glared at Douglass. 'Douglass, you can be critical of me and my pastoral work, but never, for the sake of your soul, cast doubts on those who have seen the very face of God. Those who have had such an experience have their lives marked by it and their virtuous acts laid bare before us. I believe that after such an occurrence, they can do nothing wrong.'

'I admire your faith, Reverend Marsden, but I doubt the veracity of the noble thoughts of Doctor James Hall. Only two weeks ago, I met an Australian blackfellow who told me, through his interpreter, that he had met God in Sydney. Apparently, God told him to seek out an Irish woman for a new wife and that she would look after him in every way.'

'He was lying.'

'Who? Doctor Hall?'

'Of course not. This blackfellow friend of yours. I am confident that God does not recognise either the Irish or the local natives.'

'How can you say such a thing? The native people here are humans, they have souls, the same as you and I just might have souls. Why have you ignored the locals as part of your pastoral life?'

'Because they are different. Like the Neanderthal people were different. We are human because we are created in the image of God. The blackfellows here have no reflection – they have no attachments, and they have no wants.'

'But surely they are worth saving, worth educating, worth converting to Christianity. Apart from anything else, it would make the lives of settlers much safer.'

'History will take care of that.'

'Marsden, you are honoured in New Zealand for your humanity towards the Maori people. Why such a difference in your attitude here?'

'Because the local blacks do not trade. In New Zealand, the church has established trade throughout the islands. We deal in food, timber and medicines. We buy and sell all manner of foods. We even have a trade in guns which help the Christians over there to profit from their labours. Here, the local blacks do no trade. And Douglass, let me impress on you that trade is the passageway to conversion. Soon, all New Zealand will be Christian. There is no need to confiscate Maori land. The Maori people are making their land productive and profitable. First they see profits and then, as a result of that trade, they will come to know the face of God.'

Douglass sat scrutinising Marsden as if looking for something he could believe in. 'I'm sorry, reverend, but I have distracted you from your wish to see me. I believe it was about the convict girl, Rumsby. Am I correct?'

'Perfectly correct. My wish – in truth, my demand – is that you place that convict woman in my initial care until I can arrange for her to be lodged with Doctor James Hall. He has a house available to him and requires convict labour to work. Such would free Doctor Hall for more important medical work. You will understand his needs, I am sure.'

'I think I do understand his needs. But I believe his needs are much the same as the needs of both yourself and myself. However, I cannot believe that his interests are solely concerned with domestic labour.'

'Are you suggesting that Doctor Hall has more carnal interests in that Irish convict?'

'Marsden, let us be frank with each other. We are both magistrates, so let us deal with facts. The first fact is that the convict concerned is English. She is most certainly not Irish and please, for the love of logic, why are you so antagonistic to anything or anyone who is, or may be, Irish? What have the Irish done to you?'

'Douglass, the Irish are the scourge of the British Empire.'

'In what way?'

'To start with, their adherence to the perverted religion of Roman Catholicism. They pervert the scriptures. They practise ritual cannibalism with their Holy Communion. The priest lays his hands on the chalice and claims to perform the act of transubstantion. The Catholics are told to believe that the wine and the wafers turn into the body and blood of our saviour Jesus Christ. It's witchcraft.'

'But by the same token, if you believe there is a God of creation, who is all powerful, turning wine into blood is no great achievement. I am not a Catholic, but I know many Catholics who, after they have taken part in the ritual of the Mass, feel themselves to be extremely close to God.'

'That is because they are blockheaded. Not only are they inherently stupid, but they are indoctrinated to be dangerous – in fact, murderous. And despite your protestations, I am certain that that particular convict woman you are sheltering is Irish and needs to be educated away from such a perversion.'

'And you know just the person to do that?'

'You and I both know the answer to that question. I nominate Doctor James Hall. Doctor Hall is a man of the highest integrity, a man of faith and decency, a man dedicated to the conversion of sinners.'

'And you persist in advising me to hand over my convict servant to that man?'

'Douglass I am ordering you to do so. Not only that, but I have the support of the entire bench of magistrates. They advise that the woman should be placed in the Female Factory in the short term while her transfer is organised in favour of Doctor Hall. This very afternoon, I will call at your house and take the woman in charge.'

Douglass sat opposite Marsden with just the suggestion of a smile on his face. He nodded a few times and took a big breath. 'Reverend Marsden, I can save us both some troubles. In anticipation of such a demand, I have brought the convict Ann Rumsby here to your house. I think you should have some conversation with her before you make any unfortunate decision.'

Douglass turned to Willy Bragge, still seated beside to the closed door. Willy squirmed about on his stood as if afraid of what might happen next. He didn't have to wait long.

Douglass raised his voice and gave the order. 'Bragge, please go outside and escort Ann Rumsby to me. She will have something to say to the Reverend Marsden.'

Willy Bragge stood up, staring at Douglass as if hoping he would change his mind. Douglass nodded to the door and stood waiting for his order to be filled. Willy spun around and walked quickly through the door into the sunshine. Douglass sat down again, pretending to stare at his boots while he waited. Marsden breathed heavily and calmed himself by eating another slice of pork.

Suddenly the door swung open and a nervous-looking Ann Rumsby stepped inside. Willy closed the door behind her and stayed outside with the horse.

Douglass was the first to speak. 'Please step forward, convict Rumsby. Reverend Marsden is hoping that you might be happy to be employed by Doctor James Hall. How do you feel about that? Please speak up and tell the absolute truth.'

'I don't want nothing to do with Doctor Hall.'

Marsden seemed shocked that a convict woman would speak in such a fashion. 'I remind you, convict, that you have little choice in the matter. For your sins, you were shipped to this colony as punishment. Your morals are of your race and you are described as being a whore. Doctor Hall will save you from all that.'

'He'll save me for himself. He knows I'm a virgin and he wants me in his house so that he don't get nothing after he he's had his way with me.'

'Convict,' screamed Marsden, 'stop using the word virgin. Such a state is virtually unknown in this colony.'

'I am a virgin,' she said again. Her voice was steady and she stared directly into the eyes of Marsden. 'Doctor Hall proved that I am a virgin.'

'I don't believe a word of what you say. How can you besmirch the name of Doctor Hall? You can be flogged for such accusations. So let us solve this criminal argument. We have it on paper that Doctor Hall cared for you on the *Mary Anne*. Isn't that correct?'

'Yes, that is right. He looked after me.'

'How did he do that?'

'He made me take off my clothes. Then he made me lie on the bed in the sickbay. That's when he said he had proof that I was a virgin.'

'Stop this stupid talk around the word virgin.'

'I'm happy to be a virgin. And I got Doctor Hall to thank for that. When I was lying on the sickbay bed, he had his two sailors hold me down then he stuck his finger up inside me. His finger didn't go in far, because he found that I was a virgin.'

'I'm weary of this stupidity.'

Ann suddenly threw caution to the wind and strutted past Douglass and circled to the other side of the desk. While Marsden stared at her with some disgust, she raised the hem of her long skirt to expose her ankles.

Her eyes flashed with fury. 'Here I am then, Reverend Marsden. You can find out for yourself if I am a virgin or not. Just get your finger ready. All you got to do is push it in.'

Marsden reeled back in his chair and screamed. 'Get out, woman! Lower your garment. Get out! Douglass, I order you to remove this convict!

Douglass didn't move or speak. He kept his eyes on Ann Rumsby. Ann took a step closer to Marsden and lifted her skirt higher to reveal her knees. 'Go on then. Stick your holy finger up there the same as Doctor Hall done. Push your finger in and you'll know that I am a virgin.'

'I'll have you flogged. You have insulted both me and my position as a magistrate. Douglass, remove this harridan from my house. Take her to the Female Factory forthwith.' Marsden shook as he staggered out of his chair. He stumbled backwards around the desk away from Ann, shaking his fist and ordering Douglass to remove her from the house.

While the commotion and shouting was going on, the front door was quietly opened just enough for Willy Bragge to look in and watch the rumpus. His face held a mixture of delight and fear.

Douglass noticed Willy at the door and called him in. 'Willy, help Ann out of this house and put her on the gig. We are going home.'

Ann was trembling as Willy put his hand on her shoulder and gently pushed her out of the room and into the sunlight.

Willy spoke softly to her as he helped her into the gig 'You're good at setting things on fire when you got a mind to. Don't talk till we get home and I'll get you something to eat.'

Marsden turned on Douglass with uncontrolled fury. 'Douglass, you are a blot upon this colony. You will suffer for this affront. You connive with a convict to cast evil at me. Your very soul is putrid. You will burn in the fires of Hell for all this.'

'Good God, Marsden, burning in Hell? You do go on about penal colonies.' He turned and strode to the door. He made a polite bow to Marsden and left the room, quietly shutting the door behind him. He joined the two convicts on the gig with a slight smirk on his face. He turned to Willy and nodded.

Willy shook the reins. The mare eased into the collar, spun around with the shafts and set off for home. She stepped out into a fast trot.

Ann was surprised at the change of pace. 'She's going much quicker than when we come,' she said to Willy.

'They all do that. They wants to go home, specially this one. It's where she's happy.'

'And that makes four of us,' said Doctor Douglass.

13

The Mood Changes

Ann was fascinated by the control Willy had over the mare. He didn't even flick the reins. He didn't move his arms. All he did was to tense up and quietly say, 'Easy.' On that sound, the mare tensed herself, slowed to a steady walk and stopped at the front gate. Doctor Douglass and Ann stepped down.

The doctor hurried into the house, but Ann rushed along the shafts to stand in front of the mare. She stood looking into the mare's face. She had seen many horses in Norfolk and London, but she had never noticed that horses have such big eyes. This mare had eyes like ponds of chocolate surrounded by long eyelashes. She wondered if she would be allowed to touch that big nose. She leaned forward and stroked the whole length of the mare's nose with her open hand. The mare didn't move and in that moment Ann felt herself locked into some bond with the big animal. Again she stared into the eyes of the mare and gently leaned forward until her own face muzzled with the horse. Gently, she rolled her own face round and softly kissed the side of the horse's face. She leaned back satisfied, but still wanting to stay there with her new friend.

To cover up her emotion, she called to Willy, 'Does she like folks to touch her?'

'Why not? Everyone likes to be touched – unless there be harm in it.'

'I would never harm her. Will you really help me to learn the driving, Willy Bragge?'

'No trouble. It'd be good to help with lots of things. And there'd be no harm in any of it.'

'Ann was about to shout back, 'Thanks, Teapot,' but changed it to 'That'll be good, real good.'

She laughed to herself and ran to the house while Willy walked the mare towards towards the stable. She stopped and turned to look back at Willy walking the horse to the stable and she felt a touch of surprise that he looked all right as he went. He sat up straight and, best of all at that distance, he didn't have his awful smell. She might have stood there for much of the morning, but Andrew White appeared in the doorway from inside and called her to the kitchen to help Mary scrub the kitchen floor. She still felt the dreamy sensation of having felt love for a horse. She swirled into the house telling herself that life was going to be better; that for the first time in her life she had kissed a horse and soon she was to be friends with a beautiful animal.

In the kitchen, it was obvious that Mary was unhappy. Ann walked past her and through the kitchen without speaking. She took another scrubbing brush from the curtained-off cupboard beside the back door and went back to Mary. She knelt beside Mary so that the two could scrub together. She was happy, but Mary scrubbed away as if refusing to look up.

'What's up, lover girl? You sick of scrubbing decks? I'll tell you what, this is way better than scrubbing on the *Mary Anne*.'

Still Mary wouldn't look up, so Ann swayed closer beside her friend. She looked at Mary's face and saw tears trickling down her cheeks. For a moment, she didn't know how to react.

'What's happened? You was laughing this morning before I went with the doctor.'

Mary kept her face down, but made a deep sigh as if to collect herself to receive a dark message. 'I been talking to Andrew. Did you know that in England he was going to be hanged?'

'No, I didn't. But him hanged? He must have stole something terrible big.'

'No, he didn't steal nothing. But he was in terrible trouble. The silly boy joined himself up with a mob who wanted to rise up with guns and all that and take over the government in England. Most of the leaders were hanged, but Andrew and a few more got off and he was sent out here.'

'Well, he's all right here, don't ya reckon? If he don't do nothing silly like that here, he'll better off with us here than in England. Are you frightened for him?'

'No, I'm not frightened. Although when he talks, he gets all flushed in the face and he says dreadful things against London. I'm frightened someone might be listening when he says he'd like to blow up the lot of them. Sort of Guy Fawkes.'

'Well, if you go into double harness with him, like both of you, I think you'll have a fun life of it. Are you getting any closer, the two of you?'

'We are. But I'm not the only one, that's the trouble.'

'What, he got another girl? Where'd he find one in Parramatta?'

'No, nothing like that, but the master, Doctor Douglass, he thinks that Andrew has a head full of brains. I know he's clever. He was working in England. Every day, he worked at making books.'

'What? Writing and all that?'

'No, not writing them. But I tell you what. He's wonderful at writing. He does long letters and he knows how to do them with the feather of a goose. He dips the end of the feather into his bottle of ink and he scratches words over all the pages. Oh, it's so beautiful. Your Willy Bragge, he knows the writing, but he's nothing like my Andrew.'

Ann eased back on the scrubbing, suddenly shocked. She turned to Mary, who kept on scrubbing.

'What you just say? Something about my Willy Bragge. What you mean, Mary Wooten?'

'Nothing much. But every girl needs a pal. I got Andrew White and you got Willy Bragge. Plain it is. Plain as the nose on your face.'

Ann felt her nose to be sure. She knew it was a straight nose, never been broken like many girls.

'And how is it I got Willy Bragge? I don't have nothing of him. All I got is that he's going to show me how to drive the horses, that's all.'

'That's all? Learn to drive? I'd say that's not a bad start. What's wrong with that?'

'I don't know nothing about him. Me first day here, he backhanded me face so hard, I nearly lost a good tooth. And if that wasn't enough, he kicked me all around the floor like I was a football. You think that's not a bad start. What else he got to do to me? You think he just might rip me shirt off and give me a hard flogging?'

'He won't do none of them things. Besides, he was ordered to do all that on that day by the Reverend Marsden. And Willy only pretended to hit hard. I was watching and I saw what he was up to. You should be glad of him. What's wrong with him anyway?'

'He's dreadful smelly, that's what. Doctor Douglass says the smell will go away, but I want to be pretty sure before I get close to him.'

'You got someone better up your sleeve, Annie? I think you might be in line for Doctor Hall.'

'Don't even laugh about that man. He'll be the ruin of me. He'll be thinking that if he can't be the only teapot to spout me in bed, he'll fix things to get me put six feet under. But tell me, little Mary, why you so gloomy all of a sudden? Something more to do with your clever Andrew?'

Mary couldn't bring herself to look up. Tears had started again and she shook her shoulders and stopped scrubbing and started to talk. 'A few days back everything was rosy.'

'Who's Rosy?'

'There's no girl called Rosy. But everything was rosy. Andrew was happy. I liked to be with him. I even sort of let onto him what he could put his boots under my side of our bed, if he had a mind to it.'

'Just like that? I hope he don't get lost and wander round to my side of the bed in the night. Anyway, what did he say to that?'

'He didn't say nothing. They never says nothing when things are like that. They gets all hot and steamy and either they stutter or just have trouble breathing. He just hugs me and I don't want him to ever let me go.'

'So what's wrong?'

'Well, we was talking about us being together. Like really together – all the time. Mrs Douglass, she sort of twigged what was going on and she says she would be happy to help us get married, so long as we don't do nothing in the dark before that.'

'She means you can't do nothing in bed?'

'No, she just means do nothing – anywhere at all. It's all right for them folks. They can do what they likes, whenever they likes. But the likes of us, we have to wait for someone like that Reverend Marsden to say we is married and we can do what we likes whenever we is not working. But that's not the end of it. Andrew and the doctor, they get on well and Doctor Douglass he's going to make it so that Andrew isn't a convict any more. But more than that, the doctor, he's in big with the governor and he's thinking of making a visit to London.'

Ann suddenly felt a chill at the thought of Doctor Douglass, her best defender, leaving Parramatta for England. 'When's he going?'

'Not for a while. Andrew says it might be next year, or even the year after.'

'That's a long time off. So why worry now?'

'Because the doctor wants to take Andrew with him. Might even set him up in London binding books. And if he does that, I won't never see me pal again.'

Mary began to cry again, but Ann knew that many things can change many times in a lifetime and the thought of Andrew's leaving with Doctor Douglass in a year or so brought a flood of many possible changes to herself. Her own life had changed many times since the trial in Norwich. The ship washed in a flood of horrors and it was on the ship that her real horror seeped in, in the form of Doctor Hall. A sharp pain flooded back with memories of the ship's sickbay. Luckily, a flood of pleasant sensations poured in with the memory of meeting Mrs Douglass followed by her worst horror of meeting the Reverend Samuel Marsden and the severe beating she endured from Willy Bragge. But now there existed another life-changer coming. Will Bragge was to teach her to ride and drive the horses. All she needed was freedom from the smell of him. But Doctor Douglass has said that with some care and some time, the smell and the skin trouble would pass away, that Willy Bragge could become a fine-looking young man.

'So there's no need to cry, Mary Wooten. Next year is an age away. And besides, this morning there was no frost. The sky was as blue as anyone could want and, in all that, you fell in love, or something like that, with a very handsome bookbinder, whatever that is.'

'Thank you, Annie. But you can't promise anything. We might be in chains in Port Macquarie tomorrow, mightn't we?'

'We just might, Mary. But I don't think so.'

The floor was scrubbed by the end of their conversation and the two girls changed scrubbing brushes for clean rags to do the dusting. Every item in the room had to be rubbed over and by the time they were finished, the cook set the two of them down at the small kitchen table for lunch. They were joined by Andrew. As usual, it was Irish stew with great lumps of bread. It didn't take long for the three to finish the stew and to wipe the plates clean with a new cloth. The two girls ate as much in that one meal as they might have eaten in three days on the Mary Anne. They didn't talk about the difference, but they were grateful for the change.

As soon as they finished, Andrew stood up and ladled out a big plateful. 'Ann Rumsby, take this to the stables and wait till Willy Bragge is finished. Then bring the plate back here. Mary and I will do the washing-up for the cook.'

Ann needed no persuasion, took the plate and spoon and headed off to see Willy and the mare.

Willy was mucking out the stalls, shovelling horse manure onto a heap. He laughed when he saw her coming and was happy to sit on a stool away from the steaming manure and to start eating.

Ann sat on a rock nearby secretly getting pleasure from watching him eat. 'You like that, Willy Bragge?

'It's good stuff. It's worse luck I didn't have more like it in the Old Country.'

'How's that then?'

'Well, if you got plenty of stuff to eat, you don't have to steal. Simple as that. Just a matter of kushti bok.'

'What's that then?'

'It mean good luck.'

'Is that the way they talks where you comes from?'

'Some do. It's just another lingo.'

'What's it called?'

'Rom, or Romani.'

'God help me, Willy Bragge, are you a Gypsy?'

'When it suits me. I'm not a full-blood, but it comes in handy.

'So that's how you know all about horses?

'No, I know about horses because I works with horses. That's why. You happy with that?'

'Course I am. In Norwich, I was friends with a Rom girl and her family moved about from place to place mending things and playing songs and stuff. You know many more things?'

'I'll tell you one thing. We don't like being called a Gypsy. Gypsy means from Egypt and I never been there. I'm English like you.'

'I suppose I am. I remember lots of things about my Rom friend She used to tell fortunes. She'd look at me hand and she'd tell me all about my life and how many children I can have and how one day I'd travel a lot because I'll have lots of money. Can you tell fortunes?'

'No, but seeing as you brought me something to eat, I'll show you something

'Good, but make sure there'll be no harm in it.'

Willy chuckled and moved his little stool to sit facing her. 'Show me your hand.'

Ann stretched out her hand to him, palm side up. 'Tell me something good you can see there.'

'I'll tell you. But first you have to twist your hand up facing me.' Willy took her by the wrist.

She squirmed a bit as though she had lost some control of herself.

He turned her hand, so that her palm faced his face. Then he asked her to stretch open her fingers. 'That's it, Ann Rumsby, now all your fingers is pointing to Heaven. And now you will learn that everything about you is written on them fingers.'

'How's that?' asked Ann, nervous that he might learn too much for her comfort.

'Now, I'll show you.' He said and gently took charge of her thumb. 'This thumb represents God, the most powerful finger you got and the ruler of your hand and all your life. Got that?'

Ann nodded, hoping it would all be over before Andrew or Mrs Douglass came looking for her.

Willy let go of her thumb and took hold of her index finger. 'This finger Annie, represents the king of England and all them people like the governor. This is the finger that points to everything. Your next finger represents the church and all them Catholics, chapel folk, all of them. The little finger represents someone like a Romani boy, or some boy you wish he was. It's all there. Now everyone of them stands up there in full dress. Some is coloured, some is demons, some try to do good and all that. The thing is, they all look different, sing different songs.'

'So what's it all mean?'

'It means that that's how you see it all.' Willy still held her by the wrist and with his forefinger on the other hand started to stroke down each finger into the palm of her hand. 'Now I can show you. You see all them standing up there on top of her hand, all of them looking bossy, all different, all in different uniforms. But as you go down each finger and deep into the palm of your hand, you come to a spot right in the middle where all them lines meet. And at that point all of them is the same. They all have the same worries, nightmares, daydreams and all their thinkings.'

'Not all of them. Not the Reverend Marsden?'

'Even him. He'll be there the same as everyone. All his bills will be paid in full.'

'Where's me then?'

'You're there with all of them. And you is the same. You is the woman who won't want to stand out. A woman who doesn't want to fight, but in the end is good at it.'

'How do you know all this? How do you know I don't want to fight?'

'I know you will fight. You'll fight Doctor Hall and Reverend Marsden and you'll fight all them who expects God to do their fighting for them. I'm taken with you' Ann Rumsby.'

'Well, don't be too taken. You just might be disappointed.'

Willy smiled to her and stroked her hand up as far as her elbow. 'Ann Rumsby, I'll tell you straight. In this mixed-up stuff about the past, I don't know how people live like that. They talk all the time about whens they was a kid.'

'You are right, Willy Bragge. Nowadays, I have trouble remembering Norfolk. On the ship out and here in Parramatta, I used to think about my soldier boy and the two of us walking in the park. Now if I try, I have trouble remembering his face.'

'But somethings you keep tight. I know you blame the butler for lots of things.'

'I have to. If it was the other way about, I'd have to blame meself and that'd get me nowhere.'

'Do you wonder about your mum?'

'All the time, Willy.'

'I'll tell you what, Annie. If you like, you can tell me a letter to your mum and I'll write it down for you.'

'Do you know enough words to make a letter?'

'More or less. But you'll have to be quick. If we write a letter today, 'it will take half a year before your mum gets it.

'We could tell her all the things I seen and all the thoughts that swims into my head. Sometimes I think such clever things I can't believe I thinked such things. Like I never been to school and if you don't know the writing, you can't spread your thinking about. But if you knows the writing, you can tell things to people by your writing even after you're dead.'

'Annie, don't think about being dead. It's too far away.'

'I'll try not to. But just now I knows that somehow I got to survive people like Dr Hall and Reverend Marsden. They know the writing and they will try to bring me undone.

'Don't worry, Annie, there's lots of that mob brought down good people. But they won't always win. What you got to do, Ann Rumsby, is keep in with the doctor and Mrs Douglass. Be a good worker and speak up all the time. If you do that, you got a good chance of winning in Parramatta. But take care. You are a pretty girl and that's not always a good thing for a girl. But you knows your stuff. Lots of that mob will pretend to help you. But all they want is to get under your petticoats. Now off you go.'

Ann turned and left the horse yards happy with the smell of the horses in her nose and happy to have been with Willy Bragge. She knew she was in the middle of a big change and she was happy with all of it.

The soft mood stayed with her for the next few days. But it didn't last.

14

The Cat Hangs Limp, But Waiting

Ann had tidied up the big room, dusted all the books on the wall shelves. There was nothing else to do. She stood for a few moments as if waiting for a job to appear. She couldn't just stand there, so she roused herself and stepped into the kitchen to look for Mary Wooten. But Mary had gone off somewhere with Mrs Douglass. Dr Douglass had gone off alone, driving the mare to some meeting or other.

When she looked out the window towards the horse yard, she saw Willy cleaning up the ground with a wooden shovel and she was sure he was about to start on shining up the harness. She had seen him rub sticky stuff over all the leather bits before. Then she knew he'd rub it in and when it had all gone into the leather, he would hang the tangle of harness over the horse yard rails in the sun. Finally, he would rub the harness until it shon. She could see he was a good worker.

For a few moments, she wondered what her life might be like living with him – day and night. He was gentle enough and the way he handled the horses was lovely. She brought up a picture of his fingers rubbing-in the saddle polish. She was sure he would never use his fingers in the way that Doctor Hall did. The memory made her shudder.

To take her mind off Willy and his smelly problems, she took the stiff broom and reswept the kitchen floor. She drank a glass of water from the black fountain on the stove and wiped the glass dry. She was tempted to wash the glass, but was conscious they had to save water. There was an everlasting shortage of water. They called it a drought and no one seemed to know how long it would last. She longed for rain to fill all their buckets and the tank and then she'd be able to revel in an all-over wash. She even thought of a dip in the Parramatta River. One warm afternoon, she'd seen clusters of boys and girls swimming together and splashing each other in the river, all of them laughing, shouting and swearing at the top of their voices. They were like the Gypsy kids in Norfolk. But here, life was different. Here in Parramatta, it was as if the kids actually owned the river. 'It don't matter if they is Gypsy, English, Irish or whatever. They is all of them noisy, keen on fighting and wanting to stay away from school and being nasty to them what calls themselves the high and mighty Exclusives.'

For a few moments, Ann stood still, leaning on the broom, and for some reason starting to remember the streets of Norwich, wondering if anyone back there remembered her. She wanted to go back, if only to get revenge on the butler. What revenge would she take? Just killing the man wouldn't be enough, there would have to be a lot of pain. She wondered if she could cut off his spout. Irish always called that part of a man his soup vegetables. Ann smiled at the memory of Irish on the *Mary Anne*. Irish had a story about a girl who threatened to kill her butler, so the girl, when there was no one about, tripped him onto the floor and kneeled on his chest and pushed one of the sharp kitchen knives a little bit into his stomach. He started to scream so she held the knife to his neck. That stopped him squealing and she explained that she just might cut off his spout. Apparently, he then just begged for mercy.

Ann smiled as she stood thinking of her own butler's face, all contorted, blubbering with tears and begging her not to hurt him. In her mind, she was determined not to be merciful. If he didn't have his spout, he'd never again have his way with any servant girls anywhere. But just at that point in her daydreaming, the image of him disappeared and instead there was loud banging on the front wall. She looked around for someone to answer the knocking. There was no one. She looked around for a weapon in case of robbers. But the banging continued and she walked nervously to the half-open door. Her worst fears flooded around her. Standing amid the strips of jute, Doctor James Hall looked nervous. She started to say something, but he cut her short.

'Ann, who is with you? Mrs Douglass perhaps?'

'Mrs Douglass is not here, niver is Doctor Douglass. You'd be better to come back when everyone is here. I'll tell Doctor Douglass you called to see him.'

'No need. I called to see you.'

'Please, Doctor Hall, don't cause me no trouble.

'There will be no trouble for anyone, Ann. I have come to give you the best information.'

Ann tried to talk, but Hall was nervous and he kept looking over his shoulder as if expecting trouble.

'Ann, I am here specifically to warn you of impending changes in your situation. Matters between you and myself are about to change, You are about to be made free of your present predicament. You will have no need to fear Doctor Douglass and his nasty ways.'

'I am not afraid of Doctor or Mrs Douglass. And I don't need no things changed between you and me.'

'Ann, I know your problem. I am happy to tell you that I have acquired a house in Sydney. You will be mistress of the house in charge of the other convicts and being with me. You will virtually be a free woman.'

'I will too. But I have to work off seven years first!'

'Ann, don't be afraid of the future. Soon, you will be meeting with the Reverend Marsden. Don't listen to stories about him from other convicts. Marsden is a noble man. He will do everything to help you. So please agree with everything he says. Do everything he asks of you. Understand?'

'I don't understand nothing and I don't want no meeting with your Mr Marsden. So please go.'

'Ann, I must hurry. Just remember that Marsden is your friend.' Hall spun on his heel and hurried off out the gateway heading towards Parramatta.

Ann didn't have long to daydream or stand looking. She turned and took a few strides into the big room. Suddenly she froze, spun around with fear and saw two men following her into the room. Each man had his head and face covered by a jute bag, each with holes for their eyes. She also recognised that both men wore police trousers and boots. She started to scream, but the first man held his hand up as if to quieten her. She demanded to know what they wanted. They didn't speak but advanced on her, one from behind. Ann jumped for the sideboard to get the heavy candlestick, But she never made it. The man behind her pulled out a heavy truncheon and with one hit knocked her unconscious into a crumpled heap on the floor.

'Good work. You can see she's dangerous, this one. She could have killed me. So she owes me one.'

'What she owe you?'

'Get your cuffs and put her hands together on her belly. That way she can lie out on her back.'

'Do I manacle her legs as well?'

'Don't be stupid. Just stretch her legs out. Otherwise we can't see what we want to see.'

The second man carried out his orders. Ann lay unconscious, but breathing.

The first officer carefully took hold of her ankles and stretched her legs apart. 'Now let's see what we get for all our trouble.'

The second officer removed his hood and knelt down beside the half-naked body of Ann Rumsby. He touched her on the bare thigh but quickly jerked his hand off as if afraid he might be caught doing something shameful. The first officer chuckled and began rubbing his hand where Doctor Hall had many times used his finger.

'Look, son, how long you been a constable?'

'A few weeks.'

'Then what's the worry?

'If we touch her, and Marsden finds out, he'll have me flogged. I don't want no trouble.'

'You won't get none. Just watch and learn. But first, just look at that.' He pointed to Ann's naked crotch. 'See that. That's what got her into trouble. That's what'll get her a flogging. It looks like she still got a new one. You seen one before?'

'No.'

'You got a sister?'

'Yeah, I got two. I've seen them with nothing on, but only from behind. I never seen that part of one before. It don't look like much to worry about. Can we go?'

'We go when I say and when I'm finished.'

'You going to rape her?'

'Not rape, son. She never said no, did she? The first officer was on his knees between Ann's legs and he started to unfasten the front flap on his britches. He was almost ready when they heard the crash of running footsteps.

Willy Bragge burst into the room roaring like a wild bull. 'I heard screaming. What in blazes you two up to? Ye gods, what have you done to her. If you have touched her, I'll kill the both of you. Leave her. Stand up!'

But it didn't last long. The first office pulled down Ann's petticoat and shouted orders to his offsider. 'Arrest the convict. Put the mongrel out of his misery.'

Willy Bragge was dancing about trying to get behind the pair of them. But the young officer grabbed him around the chest and tried to hold him fast. It was long enough for the first officer to snatch up his baton and bring it down on the side of Willy's head. Willy lay on the floor groaning and trying to mouth words. The two officers ignored him. Instead, they lifted Ann Rumsby, one leg each, and dragged her to the door. The police sulky stood at the gate, the horse tied to the gatepost. They lifted and dumped the unconscious Ann onto the floor of the sulky and the first officer hauled himself into the driving seat. The second officer unhitched the horse and as the first officer put the horse in motion, the young man sprang onto the footrest and stretched up and into the passenger seat. Ann's naked bottom was well on view and the young man leaned down and covered her by pulling down her petticoat.

The older man noticed and laughed. 'You know your trouble, son? You're too soft.'

As the horse lifted into a smart trot, the two men could hear Willy Bragge groaning in a loud voice.

'You going to leave him there?'

'Just this time. Next time, he'll die trying to escape. Something like that.'

15

The Chase

Apart from the Reverend Samuel Marsden, no one knew what was about to happen to Ann Rumsby. The only close member of her group who understood the cruel possibilities of the colony's legal system was Willy Bragge. Mary Wooten and Matthew White simply trembled with fear.

Mrs Douglass swirled in from the garden through the front doorway and propped. Her face changed from surprise to horror. She saw Willy Bragge, sprawled on the floor face down, rocking his head from side to side, pivoting on his nose and forehead and with blood oozing from a mess on the side of his head. Beside him knelt Mary Wooten, trying to lift his head and shoulders while constantly calling his name and urging him to wake up. Matthew White stood in the kitchen doorway open-mouthed in shock, not wanting to believe what he had seen, but frozen by the knowing that he alone could be held responsible for everything that had gone wrong.

Mrs Douglass recovered, slid her shopping onto the table and shouted at Mary, 'Where's Dr Douglass?'

Mary Wooten looked up afraid she might be in trouble. 'He's gone out, Mrs Douglass. All this musta happened when he was gone.'

'Dear God – and what musta happened?'

'Two policemen came with bags over their head, but everyone knows them.'

'What did they do?'

'They took Ann, Mrs Douglass.'

'Just like that?'

'No, Mrs Douglass. Ann was unconscious. Willy Bragge, he must have heard a lot of shouting, even from the stable. But the moment he looked in here, he saw what was happening. He roared at the top of his voice and he burst in like a mad thing. He tried to stop them from touching Ann, but one of them hit him hard with a stick and he went down. It was like he was dead. But he's alive, he's only just now waking up.'

'Matthew White, get here this instant.'

Matthew turned pale with fear and he stumbled across the room.'

'What did you see?'

'It's like Mary said. Two policemen came with disguises over their heads and they tried to get hold of Ann Rumsby.'

'Did you see her go quietly with them?'

'No, she didn't. I didn't see everything and I only saw from the back window. I wanted to see what was happening before I came in. Ann screamed and tried to fight with one of them. The old policeman, because of the silly mask, he couldn't see what he was doing. For a little while, it looked like Ann was getting the better of the old one. She really landed a few solid punches so he screamed for help from his younger one.'

'Then what?'

'The young one – everyone knows he's a bit stupid – well, he lifted his baton and hit Ann on the side of her head and that was it. She went unconscious. Willy came to the door, saw her lying there not moving. He didn't wait. He just bellowed like an angry bull and barged in. But the two of them both attacked him with their sticks. By the time I got here, Ann was out to it on the floor alongside Willy Bragge. The policemen didn't worry about Willy. They just lifted up Ann's petticoats to look at her private parts.'

'God in heaven. Did they actually try anything?'

'No. They got frightened. I made tramping noises outside and they started blaming each other and shouting at each other about Reverend Marsden. So they took hold of a leg each and dragged her out to a police cart. Her petticoats got rolled up around her neck. I saw Mary come back and I heard her screaming that there was a murder. She tried to help Willy and just after that, you saw everything yourself.'

'Where's Dr Douglass?'

'He went off in the sulky. I think he wanted to buy stuff for the house.'

'Then he'd be heading for Parramatta?'

'I'm sure he is, Mrs Douglass.'

'Then put on your running shoes and get off after him. Bring him back here as best you can.'

'Yes, Mrs Douglass. Will I tell him everything I know?'

'I hope you do. And I hope you know how to hurry.'

Matthew moved quickly to the door, waved to Mary Wooten and bounded into a fast jog down the garden path. He turned right at the gate, stretched out into a long lope and headed to Parramatta.

'It'll be Christmas before he gets there.' Mrs Douglass quietly muttered a few more expressions about any time she ever went out, something dreadful was sure to happen. But she didn't stand for long. Within moments, she was kneeling on the floor beside Willy Bragge. She managed to roll him over onto his back and held his face in her hands, rocking his head from side to side while muttering Irish swear words to bring about damnation onto the entire local constabulary. And not only that, but the entire line of Westminster governments, of English kings and to the wholly unholy and unhealthy British Empire.

Mrs Douglass didn't have time for more curses. They heard the sound of a trotting horse and the next moment, Doctor Douglass rushed into the house, knelt down and carefully looked at the damage on the side of Willy's head. He then quietly felt the bones in the back of Willy's neck. Willy groaned for a couple of moments and tried to open his eyes. At first it was little more than a flicker of his eyelids opening and shutting. Then came a deep breath and he opened his eyes to squint around the room. In the next moment, he looked at each person and murmured the word 'Ann'.

Doctor Douglass looked relaxed. 'You'll be all right, Willy Bragge. Just lie still. Mary, bring a cushion. The rest of you clean up this mess. Matthew, lead the mare up to the stable and tie her there. Unhitch the harness and sulky then give the big horse plenty of chaff and rub him down."

Mrs Douglass looked relaxed and stood up. 'What are you intending to do?'

'I'll do the best I can. I know what's on. That gunrunning preacher of ours has had Ann abducted and no doubt Docror Hall is up to his ears in this. I'll have to hurry.'

'Will you go to the courthouse?'

'Eventually. But first I must find the governor.'

'Do you know where he is?'

'No, but I'll soon find out. In the meantime, leave Willy where he is, but keep him warm. As soon as I find the governor, I'll go straight to the courthouse in Parramatta. With a bit of luck, we might be able to stop any trial.'

By the time Dr Douglass hurried to the stable, Matthew had unharnessed the mare and was feeding the Waler. He helped Dr Douglass throw the harness onto the big horse and pushed the collar over the horse's head. He buckled on the traces and led the horse out of the yard to the sulky. Matthew and Dr Douglass picked up a shaft each and backed the horse between them. Matthew then hooked the traces to the swingle bar, adjusted the blinkers and handed the reins to Dr Douglass.

The doctor stepped up into the sulky, arranged himself and touched the horse with the reins and added the command, 'Walk on.'

Slowly, the horse spun the sulky around and started off at a brisk walk towards Parramatta. They didn't walk for long. As soon as the doctor had the horse responding to the reins, he gave the order to trot and they hurried off on the rough road to Parramatta.

The doctor hadn't reached the town when he saw a man he knew from the governor's office. He pulled over and asked the whereabouts of the governor.

The man replied that he knew the governor had left some two hours ago heading to Gosford.

'Then where are you going?'

'To the courthouse. There's something on.'

'I'm sure there is,' groaned Dr Douglass. He looked anything but optimistic, but swung the sulky onto the road and headed off on the round strip, at a smart trot, to avoid Sydney and take the even rougher road north to Gosford. He passed gangs of convict road workers, some of them still in shackles, smashing rocks for gravel. None of them smiled or waved as he passed.

Two hours on the road and the horse was foaming with sweat and reduced to a walk. The hills made speed impossible and he wished he had at least two more horses. That way, they could take turns either pulling in the shafts or trotting along behind. The horse would need to drink at each creek. But the doctor didn't have another two horses so, like it or lump it, he was stuck with his situation.

Whenever he passed a hovel or house, he asked if the occupants had seen the governor. They had all seen him and all agreed he was about one hour ahead. At least he knew he was on the right road. The one more hour passed into the second.

Half an hour later, he saw ahead a coach and four horses. The horse managed to lift into a trot and with a bit of hailing and urging, Dr Douglass overtook the governor.

It didn't take long to explain the abduction of Ann Rumsby. The governor practically lost his temper and turned for home. Douglass sat with the governor, allowing one of the postilions to hold the reins of Doctor Douglass's horse over the back. The waler was relieved and picked up speed. The five horses cantered whenever the road was level. The carriage had brakes which removed the weight of the carriage, making it easy for the horses to trot downhill. On level ground, they made great speed. But for all that, they didn't arrive in Parramatta until late in the afternoon. There was no excitement in Parramatta, only the sounds of convict workmen repairing main streets and building new houses.

Well into the day, Dr Douglass and the governor were urging the horses towards Parramatta.

Much earlier than that, Ann slowly regained consciousness. She squinted around the cell, wondering where she was and what horror could happen next. Her head throbbed. Her neck was stiff and, whenever she moved, a sharp pain speared up into the back of her head. The blood had dried around her right ear and her hair was stiff with blood halfway down her neck. She gingerly touched the wound with her fingers and winced. There was no new blood oozing out, but she had no way of washing away the blood that had dried. Her situation was worse even than her time in the cells near London. All around her now there hung nothing but a curtain of silence. She sat on the floor, her back against the wall and her face cradled on her knees. But not for long.

She heard men talking loudly not far from her cell door. Footsteps approached, there was a rattle of keys and her door was flung open.

A policeman walked into the room, stepped across and prodded her bottom with his boot. He ordered her to stand. Ann swung herself onto her knees and with both hands on the cell wall clambered upright. She faced the policeman and he ordered her to extend both hands. She knew what he meant and presented both arms in front. The policeman flicked on the handcuffs and screwed them tight.

'Your head's still feeling tight, eh? But don't worry too much, you'll wash up all right. And if I had my way, I'd find somewhere else to make you feel nice and tight all over.'

'And if you had your way, it would be the last thing you'd do on this Earth.'

The policeman didn't say anything more, but flicked his head towards the door and walked out. Ann stumbled along behind him, down the short corridor and into the court house.

The moment she entered the room behind the policeman, a quiet clapping broke out. The public seats were full and many men whistled at the sight of her.

Doctor Hall stood up from the front row. He saw her bruised face and her bloodied hair. His mouth sagged open in shock. 'Marsden?' he bleated. 'What have you done?'

The Reverend Marsden sat in his central seat on the bench with five other magistrates flanked beside him. 'We have done nothing, Doctor Hall. This female convict has given this colony many problems. Getting her here was just another such problem.'

'What happened?'

'On your request, Doctor Hall, we sent two officers to bring her to this court. As you can see, she is a violent person with a dangerous character. She even had to be subdued several times on the road from the house of Doctor Douglass to this court. Now allow me the right to question the officer. Officer!'

The policeman came to attention and nodded to the bench.

'Officer, did you have trouble with the witness?'

'Yes, your worship. She fought like a tiger and we had to use force.'

'You say we. How many were you?'

'Three, your worship – myself, my junior constable and the police driver. It took two of us to control her.'

'And is the other constable here as a witness?'

'No, your worship. The young man is still in the hospital.'

'Yet another victim of rum?'

'No, your worship. In the middle of the night, he was crossing the park on his way home when he was set upon by one man and rendered senseless. He was found by a passer-by who called a cab and he was taken to hospital. We believe he will recover.'

Ann mouthed the word 'Pity.'

Marsden stared around the room and came to concentrate his gaze on Ann Rumsby. 'I suspect that this female has played some part in your constable's misfortune. It's a pity that those in authority are blissfully unaware of the dangers that exist in this colony. I notice that the female witness is smiling over your constable's misfortune. What has the female to say on this matter?'

Ann straightened up, glared with hatred at Marsden and spoke with a clear voice. 'All I can say is that that policeman thumped me many times in the cart. Even when they brought me here, I was given a few more punches. They dragged me down the corridor and pushed me onto the floor in the cell. They came in with me and I got kicked in the head and on me behind.'

'You have a witness?'

'No, you know I don't.'

Laughter broke out and Marsden ordered the court to be silent.

Marsden asked Doctor Hall to address the bench.

Doctor Hall stood quietly unable to look at the mess the police had made of Ann Rumsby. He spoke quietly and was seen to be shaking. He stood silent until a man softly called out the name 'Sticky Fingers'. This was followed by quiet chuckles and again Marsden ordered silence.

Hall started quietly. 'I stand before you all as a man who has always tried to serve his country. I was given the responsibility of surgeon on our convict ships, to not only care for the physical health of the women convicts, but also to take on the added responsibility of bringing about a reformation of character in each of the women. I took it as my duty to lead them gently to God. I saw in today's witness, this female convict, Ann Rumsby, a person capable of reform and of eventually being able to walk in the presence of God and to look upon the face of our-Lord Jesus Christ. I took her conversion as my sacred duty and my highest obligation. In my affidavit, I have suggested a series of question for the bench and I hope that when this trial is done, you will find that I have done my duty to God and not only to God, but to my country and to this convict and all the female prisoners in my charge.' With that, he sat down, desperately trying not to look at Ann Rumsby.

Marsden sat reading quietly for a few moments then glared at Ann and asked her to recall some of the events that took place on the ship *Mary Anne*.

Ann nodded her agreement and Marsden began what was to become one of Australia's most tortuous trials.

'Convict Rumsby, were you ever sick on board?'

'Yes.'

'Were you in the hospital?'

'Yes,'

'Do you recollect being frightened in the night, whilst in the hospital?'

'I do not recollect that I was. '

'Do you recollect a woman named Ellerbeck being punished?'

'Yes, I do.'

'How was she punished?'

'She was handcuffed to another girl and kept on bread and water.'

'What had she done?'

'She was caught on deck in the night.'

'Was that all?'

Ann didn't want to explain more details, but following more questions from other member of the bench and being warned that her liberty could depend on her telling 'the whole truth', she spoke out.

'She was found on deck naked with a half-naked sailor.'

This further information brought more humorous murmurs from the public seats.

Marsden immediately warned the public that if they interfered in the trial, they would be expelled from the courthouse. He then returned to interrogating Ann. 'Please tell the bench, how did our Doctor Hall learn that female convict Ellerbeck was not in the prison?'

'I was taken ill in the night and the other prisoners sent for the doctor. He came straight away.'

'Was he kind to the female Ellerbeck?'

'Yes. He even kissed her.'

'Was Doctor Hall in the habit of kissing some of the young women after their punishment and if they were sorry for their offence?'

'Yes.'

'Let us be clear. When you were taken ill, Doctor Hall went down to the convict quarters straight away and it was then that another woman told him that Ellerbeck was out.'

'Yes.'

There were murmurs of approval from the public and Marsden again glared them into silence.

'Convict Rumsby, according to your affidavit, two of the women told Doctor Hall that Ellerbeck was free and was cavorting with a sailor up on the deck. Is that so?'

'Yes. Some of them women were jealous. They dobbed her in. I think they wanted to get the doctor down to us, because they liked the way he touched them.'

'Disgusting. How long were the two women handcuffed together?'

'I can't say exact. But it was several days.'

'Where were you when the handcuffs were taken off Ellerbeck?'

'I was in the hospital.'

'Was it daytime? Or night?'

'I think it was in the eight bells, about midnight.'

'Explain to us what took place at that time.'

'I saw Ellerbeck pushed into the hospital. She was crying and I saw Doctor Hall speak to her. I don't know what he said, but whatever it was, she just fell to her knees and started to say prayers. Doctor Hall stayed with her and sometimes he spoke to her. I couldn't hear what either of them said because she was crying all the time. She upset me.'

'Did you tell Doctor Hall that you were upset by the way she was treated?'

'Yes, I did.'

'Now, be very clear. You say you saw Doctor Hall kiss the convict Ellerbeck.'

'Yes.'

'Did Doctor Hall ever kiss you in the hospital?'

'No.'

'Was Doctor Hall a man who behaved to you like a father or a man who wished to seduce you?'

After a few moments in which Ann looked unsure as to how she might answer, she mumbled the words, 'Like a father.'

Again there were more quiet chuckles from the public which Marsden ignored. He sat like a rock, staring down at his notes and the affidavit supplied by Doctor Hall. Ann shuffled about on her feet trying to scratch the dried blood from her frizzy hair. A couple of the five magistrates pretended to cough as to break Marsden's spell. He looked up and again fixed his eyes on Ann Rumsby. For a moment, he seemed uncertain of what to say.

Finally he spoke out. 'Convict Rumsby, did Doctor Hall ever take indecent liberties with you?'

'No.'

'What presents did you receive from Doctor Hall on board the ship?'

'Several books.'

'What kind of books?'

'Religious books.'

More chuckles from the public.

Marsden pushed on. 'What was the last present you received from Doctor Hall since you left the ship?'

Ann paused for a moment and her answer brought loud laughter. 'Ten shillings.'

Someone in the gallery whispered about Ann being expensive.

One of the magistrates commented that ten shillings was a lot of money. Marsden ignored both the public laughter and his fellow magistrate's comments.

'Ann Rumsby, tell the court, why did Doctor Hall give you ten shillings and what did he say when he gave it to you?'

'I can't say why, but I think he gave it to me because of my good behaviour on the ship.'

'Could Doctor Hall have had any other motive other than that of rewarding your good conduct?'

'No.'

'Did Doctor Hall mention the possibility of any more money?'

'He said a pound or two.'

'Are you quite sure of that?'

'Yes.'

'Tell the court, where you both were when he gave you the ten shillings?'

'We was down the Sydney Road, past the Western Road.'

'When you were at the house of Doctor Douglass, did you ever see Doctor Hall and my fellow magistrate Sir John Jamison? And, if you did, how long did that meeting last?'

'I think it was a bit more than a fortnight ago.'

'Did they speak to you? And if so, what was said?'

'Sir John Jamison asked me if Doctor Douglass was at home. I told him that Doctor Douglass was gone off to Sydney.'

'After that, did Doctor Hall speak to you?'

'Yes.'

'What did he say?'

'I don't know what his words was.'

'What do you think was said?'

'I understood that he wanted me to come to him and he'd look after me. But I can't remember exactly.'

A ripple of laughter spread around the public seats. Marsden was affronted by the meaning of the laughter.

'Where was all this said?'

'First in the factory, and then in the house of Dr Douglass. Doctor Hall was standing just inside the front door. After that, he left.'

'Then what happened?'

'After a while, I changed me mind and I ran down to the gate and took off after him.'

'Did you walk, or run?'

'I don't remember. I probably ran. But in the end I cached up with him about halfway to the turnpike on the Sydney Road.'

'Where was the last place you saw Doctor Hall before that day?'

'In the factory.'

'How long ago was that?'

'I was in the factory for one month before I moved to the house of Doctor Douglass. So it was sometime then. But I don't know what day it was.'

'At the factory, what did Doctor Hall say?'

'He talked to the women.'

'What do you think was the object of Doctor Hall's visit?'

'He gave some little money to the prisoners so they could buy biscuit.'

'Where in the factory did this exchange of biscuit money take place?'

'He was just inside the gate.'

'And did he speak to you on that particular day?'

'Yes.'

'And what did he say?'

'He was surprised that I was still there in the factory.'

'Did Doctor Hall have any further communication with you after that day?'

'No.'

'Did you hear of Doctor Hall being in Parramatta after that?'

'Yes.'

'On what occasion was that? And where did you hear that he was?'

'I was told that a big party of gentlemen was having a grand dinner in Parramatta and that Doctor Hall was there with them.'

'Who told you that Doctor Hall was there?'

'My fellow servant Matthew White. He was told to work there at the dinner.'

'Did you ask White to speak to Doctor Hall?

'No. But I told White it was me who wanted to speak to Doctor Hall.'

'On his return, did you ask White why he did not speak to Doctor Hall?'

'Yes, but he said he couldn't speak to Doctor Hall. So I never asked him about it.'

'Let us return to the Sydney Road. On that day when you met with Doctor Hall, did you tell him you were soon to leave the house of Doctor Douglass?'

'Yes. On that day I told him I was soon to go to the house of Judge Field.'

'Who told you that such a move might happen?'

'Doctor Douglass.'

'Did you tell Doctor Hall that Mrs Field wanted you in her household?'

'Yes.'

'Then, did you tell Doctor Hall you also wished to move to the house of Mrs Field?'

'Yes.'

'Did you ask Doctor Hall to help your going to join Mrs Field? And why did you ask such a thing of Doctor Hall?'

'Because I thought he could be my friend.'

'Did you subsequently receive a letter from Doctor Hall? And, if so, how many days after your meeting on the Sydney Road?'

'Some days, maybe a week or so.'

'Who gave you the letter?'

'Mr Thorn, the chief constable.'

'Did you read the letter?'

'No. You know I can't read.'

'Then what did you do with it?'

'I gave it to Matthew White so he could read it for me.'

'Do you remember anything from that letter about a pious gentleman?'

'Yes, I do.'

'What was that gentleman's name?'

'Mr Marsden.'

'And what was written about this Mr Marsden?'

'It said that Mr Marsden would protect me. Something like that.'

Marsden said nothing, but turned to the other magistrates and nodded his agreement with what had been said. They all repeated the action like a row of nodding puppets. With that consensus, Marsden again turned to Ann Rumsby. By that time, the trial had lasted more than four hours and seemed it would go on forever. Many of the public grew tired of the inquisition and quietly went home.

'Convict Rumsby, let me remind you that you are not here charged with any offence. You are here to support the bench in our duty to affirm the affidavit given to the court by Doctor Hall. Do you understand that?'

Ann gave the impression that she was uncertain as to what she could, or should, say. She managed a very weak 'Yes.'

'Convict, you received another letter from Doctor Hall. What did he say in that letter?'

'That I should write down everything that had happened to me since I arrived in the colony.'

In the case which followed, Marsden tried to force Ann to confirm the accusation by Doctor Hall that Doctor Douglass had on several occasions taken liberties with her body. Ann shook her head in denial, but stated that Doctor Douglass and Mrs Douglass had both advised her to marry Willy Bragge. Ann explained that she was not happy to marry Willy Bragge and thought that such a marriage would be the ruin of her.

'Did Willy Bragge want to marry you?'

'He might've. You'll have to ask him.'

'What did you have against Willy Bragge?'

'He's a teapot.'

'Have you told this to Willy Bragge?'

'No.'

'Why not?'

'Because he never asked me such a thing.'

'Do you wish to be a married women?'

'Why would I? What would there be in being married for me, or for any girl? I would just be a sort of slave, working me body to the bone for him and all that time just lugging a bellyful of arms and legs year after year. A sort of stud farm.'

'Convict Rumsby, I detect in you a vulgarity which is Irish. You cannot explain any concept without being vulgar. I find you a disgusting person. Not only that, but it is impossible for you to be honest at any time. You were given an opportunity in this trial to honour your protector, Doctor James Hall, and the opportunity to describe the crudity of your conduct with Doctor Douglass. I have considered this case very carefully and I can clearly find you guilty of lying under oath. Therefore, I pronounce you guilty of perjury and in an effort to help you atone for your copious sins against God and this court, I sentence you to seven years hard labour in the penal colony of Port Macquarie.

Ann staggered in the box, dumbfounded. Before she could utter a word, the old policeman grabbed her arm and dragged her from the court, back to her cell.

The court was stunned. The other magistrates started to mumble and decree that the sentence was just and necessary. The word whore was mentioned several times. The public simply sat silent, their sympathies swelling with Ann Rumsby.

Marsden ordered the court closed and along with the other magistrates hurried from the building. As he left, he called the constable to guard the papers. On no account could they be touched until he returned within the half hour. The constable made a vague salute and watched the departure of the magistrates. He then sat quietly on the end seat next to the exit and began slowly and methodically to swig from a small bottle of rum. With the courthouse empty and being the only policeman on duty, he sat to quietly enjoy the power of his solitude and the thought of what his chances were with the female convict locked in the cell.

However, the sudden explosion of the governor along with Doctor Douglass through the front door spoiled his drink. He jumped to his feet and tried to look busy, picking up papers, shuffling the pages and, putting them down again. He looked even more frightened when the governor barked a command.

'Officer, collect all the papers from the magistrates' bench and bring them to me.'

'I'm sorry, your excellency, but Mr Marsden ordered me to leave everything while he went off for a short break.'

'Then you would prefer a flogging for disobeying my orders?'

The policeman saluted and hurried to the bench, collected all the papers, took them to the governor and saluted again. 'Please, your excellency, you will tell Mr Marsden I did this at your bidding.'

'I think I will tell your Mr Marsden many things. In the meantime, return to your barracks for one hour.'

The policeman saluted yet again, spun on his heel and marched from the courthouse.

The governor and Doctor Douglass sat beside each other on one of the public benches near the doorway.

The governor quickly sorted the papers from all the five magistrates and settled on a rough summary of the depositions of the case conducted by Samuel Marsden. After reading silently for several minutes, he sat back and relaxed. All he said was 'Well, well, well.'

Doctor Douglass was curious. 'Find something?'

'My dear Douglass, I think I have found everything. Now all we need to do is patiently wait until the Reverend Marsden runs back here with his policeman.'

'You think he will hurry?'

'He will. Five minutes after I dismissed our police officer and he left this building, half the population of the entire colony will have known that I have interfered in the sacred work of Marsden and all his acolytes. We can watch with royal interest.'

The governor had hardly spoken when the magistrate, the Reverend Samuel Marsden burst through the doorway with the same policeman, ignored the governor and Douglass and rushed to the bench.

The moment he saw that all his papers were gone, he turned on the governor. He bowed slightly as if to advise that the battle had begun. 'Your excellency. I can not believe that you have taken my papers and depositions. If so, I would have them returned to me this moment.'

'Mr Marsden, I am afraid I will do no such thing. But I will say that I have found your work here this morning more than interesting.'

'Your excellency, I demand the return of my official papers. You have no business to interfere in the running of the court.'

'Mr Marsden, I have read your findings of the Ann Rumsby case and I presume she is here somewhere in this court. Am I right?'

'The convict Rumsby is certainly here. She will remain here under protection of the court until transport leaves for Port Macquarie. I am confident that will occur within the next day or so.'

'Mr Marsden. You have found this convict guilty of perjury. How is this so?"

'It is perfectly clear, even to a man such as yourself, who is not experienced in matters of the law, that the convict concerned has lied under oath.'

'I see that here in your findings. But in what matter did she actually lie under oath?'

'Your excellency, she had supplied the court with an affidavit. However, in court under examination she denied almost every clause in the said document.'

'Did the convict actually write the affidavit?'

'Your excellency, she did not. It was written for her by Doctor James Hall.'

'How interesting. And did she know the contents of the affidavit before being brought to court?'

'She was not asked such a question. She would not have told the truth anyway. The woman is a felon.' Marsden was increasingly angry and determined to defend his judgment.

The governor was equally determined to continue his own interrogation. 'Mr Marsden, I am afraid you have overreached your authority as a magistrate. In fact, I am quite certain that you and your bench of magistrates have all exceeded your jurisdiction in delivering findings on this alleged crime for which you have no authority. You have found the convict guilty of perjury. However, as she did not write the affidavit, nor have such a document read to her before the trial, it is obvious that no perjury has been committed. It is not she who lied, but he who wrote the affidavit. My dear Marsden, what do you say to that?'

Marsden began to bluster with temper. 'If I-myself had my own personal way, I would have the woman flogged, front and back, before sending her off.'

'I'm sure you would. I'm sure you would even enjoy such a sight. But I will save you from that folly because I know that your exclusive bench of magistrates have no authority in law to try anyone for the crime of perjury. It is quite without the law for you to conduct such a trial. Besides, in this case there is no perjury committed whatever. So the woman has committed no crime.'

'Your excellency, this will bring about a break down in law and order throughout this colony. Please be guarded in your words, your excellency.'

'Thank you for your advice. But I am curious, Mr Marsden. How will the acquittal of your convict woman break down law and order throughout the colony?'

Marsden was shaking with barely controlled anger and he spoke with some difficulty. 'Your excellency, if you continue to demand that you alone can demand who can be tried and in what line of the law the convict is to be tried, we will bring down a reign of terror about your ears, your excellency.'

'And how, Mr Marsden, do you propose to bring this reign of terror down upon me?'

'It will not only be upon you, your excellency, but upon the entire colony.'

'And how do you intend to do just that?'

'Your excellency, you must be aware that law and order in this colony is served by the bench of magistrates. We are the law.'

The governor sat quietly, then leaned back and took a deep breath. He looked into the eyes of Magistrate Marsden. 'Mr Marsden, I will ask you to first release your innocent prisoner from her cell and and have her brought here before me.'

Marsden tried to swallow his anger. 'I will do no such thing. The convict Rumsby has been found guilty of perjury and is to be sent to Port Macquarie, where she will be given the redeeming task of working in hard labour for the next seven years. She will eventually become an accepted citizen of this colony.'

'I must tell you, Mr Marsden, that you are wrong both in law and charity. The woman has committed no crime whatever.'

Marsden's voice lifted into a scream and his face looked like it must burst. 'There is the affidavit,' he shrieked. 'The affidavit, the affidavit. She had to swear to the affidavit.'

'Mr Marsden, there is no value or validity in this so-called affidavit. There was no perjury, no crime. And to order a convict to suffer seven years of hard labour in a cruel settlement where she will be available to any bully and a string of rapists, gives you no honour whatever. What do you say to that?'

Marsden opened his mouth as if to scream. His body shook and his face flushed with a flood of sweat. 'Your excellency,' he yelled, 'there is no possibility of any reconciliation between you and the bench of magistrates. You are prepared to free a criminal, liar and a whore. You defy the bench in such a way that we cannot possibly continue to work under your governorship.

'Then, Mr Marsden, you can't bring yourself to work under my jurisdiction? If so, you must resign. Is it just you or your other exclusives on the bench?'

'We all resign forthwith. There will be no law in this colony.'

'Mr Marsden, before witnesses, I accept your resignation of the entire bench of magistrates.'

'Who will conduct the court?'

'My dear Marsden, that is of no importance to you. From this moment on, you are not a magistrate in this colony. I suggest you reserve all your profound energies to conducting, weddings and funerals. So, for now, you are dismissed.'

Marsden turned and stumbled in his anger, to turn at the door.

'Your excellency. You have made a grave blunder. You will be hearing much more of this. You will be miserably sorry for your illiterate actions.'

'Don't waste your breath, Mr Marsden. Goodbye and I wish you well.'

Douglass sat as if dumbfounded. But not for long. The initial policeman walked in and stared at the governor and Douglass. He looked as if he had something to say. but was cut short.

'Constable, please go to the cells and bring up the female convict, Ann Rumsby.'

The policeman looked nervous. 'I can do that, your excellency, but she is a trouble. A terrible trouble. It took three of us to get her in the cell.'

'I am sure you will have no further worry, constable. Please go now.'

The policeman pushed the corridor door open and returned a few moments later with Ann shackled by the ankles and in handcuffs. She tried to smile when she saw Dr Douglass but the pain in her head stopped the smile halfway.

The governor was shocked by the sight of Ann Rumsby. He had only known her as a beautiful young girl in the house of Doctor Douglass. He ordered the constable to attention.'

'Constable, remove all that ironwork. This woman will be a free woman, with a full pardon, by tomorrow morning. So as far as I am concerned, she is a free woman this minute.'

The constable shook a little, not knowing who was really in charge.

'Don't worry, constable. The entire bench of magistrates has resigned. From now on, you take orders from me. And of course I will ask Doctor Douglass to help out.'

Both Doctor Douglass and the constable looked surprised. Douglass looked strangely happy. The constable moved slowly to remove the shackles and Ann sat on the nearest bench looking dazed. Her hand went to her wounded head and she winced.

She spoke very slowly. 'If this is the law in this country, I don't think much of it. Irish always said we'll have to make new rules and send the fat ones back to London.'

Doctor Douglass chuckled and looked squarely at Ann Rumsby. 'I am sure your Irish friend is right.' He was cut short in whatever else was he wanted to say.

There were more footsteps followed by Mrs Douglass and Willy Bragge. Willy wore a tight bandage around the top of his head and a sheepish grin on his face.

The governor welcomed Mrs Douglass and questioned Willy Bragge. 'How did your injury come about, convict? I suspect our over-seer Mrs Douglass had a hand in it.'

Willy Bragge stood a little unsteady and Mrs Douglass helped him take a seat.

She nodded to the governor and her husband. 'I did the bandage,' she said quietly.

Doctor Douglass was the first to jump into the conversation, 'And you did it very well.'

She laughed. 'I'm glad you approve. I think I could have been a very good doctor myself. But of course I'm not a teapot.'

Everyone laughed. All except Ann, who managed a weak smile as if still unsure of her future.

She looked towards Mrs Douglass. 'What does that word pardon mean? Is it sort of good manners?'

'Can be,' said Mrs Douglass. 'But I am sure that in this case, it will mean you are no longer a convict. You will be a free woman, just like me, as soon as you get your papers. There will be many people you will want to tell about your change of station?'

'I can think of lots. But first I want to tell me mother. She will be worried about me. And then I will write to the butler and I'll tell him that if he comes to this place I will get him as a cleaner of toilets, till the day he dies. But then again, I probably won't. People like him, they live their lives up to their necks in trouble.'

The governor came to attention and stood up. 'My dear Douglass,

I will be glad if you would come to Government House tomorrow and I will have the papers prepared for Ann Rumsby. Next, we will discuss a pardon for Willy Bragge. And then we can talk, at last, about this idea you have of creating a university. I know there are several people who thoroughly like the idea. Have you thought of a title for such an ambitious establishment?'

'What is wrong with the University of Sydney?'

'Wonderful, It will become another bright spot in the Empire.'

Turning to Ann, he said, And you, Ann Rumsby, you will be the spark that has ignited a wonderful legacy. Ann Rumsby, you have helped to bring about a university. We will all be proud of you. What do you think of that?'

'There's a couple of things I gotta do before I can think of such a thing.'

'Tell us your demands.'

'I needs to have a wash and get all this blood off of me neck and then I'll have to sit and learn to read and write. I'll need to read a book that's not the Bible.'

Mrs Douglass clapped her hands with delight. 'Your excellency, I hope I may accompany my husband to Government House tomorrow. I want to see Ann's name written in bold letters.'

'Mrs Douglass, you will be muchly welcome.'

With that, he saluted the empty bench and strode from the building. He gave the appearance of a man who was well pleased with a good day's work.

With a bit of shuffling of places and concerned talk about tomorrow, it was decided that Dr Douglass and Mrs Douglass would drive themselves home, leaving Willy to accompany Ann as soon as she felt fit to travel. The Douglasses left, leaving Willy and Ann sitting face to face in the courthouse.

Ann rolled her eyes, looking around the room. She seemed to have difficulty finding something to say. Finally she spoke. 'Willy Bragge, today you don't smell so bad.'

Willy blushed and swallowed. 'I'm well pleased to hear that. Anything else?'

'Well, now that I is about to become a free woman and you is a convict servant, can I drive the mare home?'

'I'm happy to go along with that. But I should tell you sort of plain, it's only married folk who drive together.'

'I think you is telling butler sort of stories. Besides, I know you is already married to someone else. I'm sure that's right, isn't it?'

'If you say so.'

'Well then, how can you be married again?'

'Because this is another country. And it's like they say, you get married on land. But if you goes more than three miles out to sea, you is single again.'

'You thinking of going to sea again?'

'No, I baint. One trip like that's enough. I's here for keeps.'

'Don't you need to get a divorce before you marry again?'

'They reckon. But a divorce costs a fortune. No one here can afford it. So no one does it. The people just get married again and they stays married to that one, until they dies.'

'So, you got any little Bragges running around somewhere?'

'I think there's only three. One before and two after.'

'Before and after what?'

'Before and after we was married.'

'And you never tried to get in touch? You know how to read and write.'

'I tried for a few years, but all that was a long way away. I just hoped I could start again if ever I got free of being a convict.'

'If we was to marry, Willy, would you want to spread yourself about a bit more, have a little Bragge to look after?'

'Ann Rumsby, you make all sorts of conditions.'

'I don't, but I should. I got to be careful with teapots. They only think about things for five minutes at a time. They want to share their spout about and don't care what happens afterwards. It's like they say —

if you is born with a split instead of a spout, there's nowt good can come of it.'

'Be that all that you can say of it?'

'No, I thought a lot about it over the past few days. I's had lots of trouble with teapots. That Doctor Hall, he wanted to get me into bed because he knew there was nowt wrong with me down there. But he didn't want to marry me. He just wanted to have fun with me down there and later on, back in England, marry a fancy sort of woman with servants. And if his wife has girl servants, he'll help himself to that lot as well. Even the butler, he used to help himself. But I needs protection. A woman who is married to a good man is sort of closed off from most teapots. Other teapots has to keep their britches buttoned up out of harm's way.'

'So what do you say?'

'I will think about it on the way home – if I can drive some of the way. And if I say yes, how will we do it?'

'We arrange for the wedding banns to be read in the church for a week or so and then we turn up with a couple of people who will be what they call witness for us.'

'Like Doctor and Mrs Douglass?'

'Perfect, and we arrange a sort of party afterwards and that night we sleep together and that'll be it.'

'Just like that. But we won't sleep, will we? We'll do that a lot.'

'If that's what you want.'

'First, I want to know how I should do it. I don't want nuffing like Doctor Hall and his fingernails. If we do things, I only want you with your spout. And only if you're gentle. Is all that right?'

'Why don't we just let things be? Let us find our own way. What do you say now?'

'I say let's drive home and tonight we might just try doing that, just a little bit, to make sure we are right for each other.'

'You will become famous, Ann Rumsby. I will be proud to be your husband.'

'I won't be famous and I don't want such a thing anyway. Samuel Marsden is famous and look at him. Everyone hates him. Doctor Hall wants to be famous and everyone uses him. He's just a frightened man. And I hate him as well. The butler was a snivelling creep of a man and I'd piddle all over him. But you, Teapot Bragge, you are honest. You must be one of the few honest teapots in this country. I think I will have to trust you. So, before I drives us home, I will say yes to all your funny questions. How's that?'

'That's fine by me. Ann Rumsby. That's sure fine by me.'

Epilogue

Governor Brisbane kept his word. A few days following the infamous court case, Ann Rumsby received a full pardon. For the rest of her life in Australia, she was a free woman. She learned, with Willy's help, to drive and ride horses.

A short time later, Willy Bragge also received a full pardon on account of his good behaviour and his ability to read and write. He was given a position of constable. He remained in the police force for the remainder of his working life and finally was the officer in charge of a district station. He also worked as an apothecary. With the 'exclusive' bench of magistrates in involuntary retirement, Brisbane hastened the arrival of Australia's first chief justice, Sir Frances Forbes, to Sydney. Forbes introduced trial by jury, ending the vicious reign of the Reverend Samuel Marsden and his 'exclusive' acolytes.

Ann Rumsby and Willy Bragge were married according to the rites of the Anglican Church. Marsden was not invited to perform the ceremony. Over the time of their married life, Ann and Willy were reported to be a happy couple. Ann refused any limelight, expanded her contempt of any misogyny, and renewed her interest in needlework. She maintained Willy's uniforms in immaculate condition.

Together, despite Ann's earlier reservations, they had eight children. Ann died in 1850, many years before Willy, and their two graves lie side by side in St Annes Anglican churchyard, Ryde, NSW.

Dr James Hall continued to cause trouble and was eventually ordered to leave the colony.

Dr Henry Grattan Douglass and William Wentworth together strove to establish the University of Sydney. That institution stands as an honour to both men.

The Reverend Samuel Marsden (1708–1838), bore ill will against Ann Rumsby, Willy Bragge and Dr Douglass most of his life. In retirement, he gave much of his energies to farming and profiteering throughout the Pacific.

Governor Brisbane has an Australian capital city named in his honour.

About the Author

Brian Hungerford, an Australian of Irish descent, has an overwhelming passion for the study of anything Australian. It started young and, after eleven schools and some fourteen homes, he set about a lifelong study of Australian history.

A prodigious writer over many years, most of Brian's early income came from dramatised radio features, short stories and journalism.

In 1959, along with his wife and son, he took ship to Spain and spent most of a year writing insights into Spanish rural life and studies on the Spanish guitar.

His next stop was the World Service of the BBC, where he poured out screeds of stories and articles on British agriculture. He was so successful he was seconded to the United Nations Organisation to teach broadcasting in countries of Central America. These included Cuba, Mexico, Costa Rica, Panama, Jamaica and Trinidad and Tobago. All in Spanish.

Next he continued his interest in broadcasting with a period in Turkey, after which he served the UNO (FAO) for some twenty years in PNG, Bangladesh, Western Samoa. Malaysia, Sri Lanka (twice) and finally Zambia.

In 1985, he returned to Australia and settled in Canberra, to devote himself to short stories, two novels and a three-act play on the life of Ann Rumsby. He had fallen in love with Ann Rumsby in 1955, while he was researching a radio feature on Louisa Lawson, mother of Henry. In London, he continued his research into Ann Rumsby in the British Museum.

He now lives in Canberra with his Spanish wife, Luisa Espino Granado, scribbling endless stories and playing Irish, Scottish and Spanish bagpipes.